# SHADOWS OF THE PAST

Still-Life with Shape-Shifter
The Turning Season

**Young adult novels**
The Safe-Keeper's Secret
The Truth-Teller's Tale
The Dream-Maker's Magic
General Winston's Daughter
Gateway

**Standalones, Collections, and Graphic Novels**
Angels and Other Extraordinary Beings
Heart of Gold
Jenna Starborn
Quatrain
Shadows of the Past
Shattered Warrior
Summers at Castle Auburn
The Shape-Changer's Wife
Wrapt in Crystal

# Shadows of the Past

Sharon Shinn

*Shadows of the Past*

# Table of Contents

# INTRODUCTION

It's common wisdom among writers that stories are sparked by one of two events: a person leaving on a journey, or a stranger arriving in town. While these themes show up often in my own work, there's another one that I rely on a lot: forcing a character to deal with the turmoil of the past.

The way the past shapes the present is a pretty consistent theme in the seven short stories in this collection. Some of the men and women here are facing up to painful memories; some are finally taking responsibility for previous actions; some are just dealing with loss. All of them hit a pivotal moment where they figure out how to move forward.

Three of the stories are murder mysteries. These can be challenging to write in the close confines of a short story, because each one has to contain a murder, a cast of potential killers, and an elegant solution, in a very few pages! But in each case, I was invited into anthologies I really wanted to be part of, and I had a great deal of fun putting the pieces together.

In "The Sorcerer's Assassin," decades' worth of spite and envy spill over when one of the professors at a school for magic is found murdered—and the only suspects are the fellow mages who have always hated him. The story was published in 2004 in *Powers of Detection,* a mystery-and-fantasy anthology edited by Dana Stabenow.

"In the House of Seven Spirits" is about a writer named Erica who takes possession of a haunted house for the summer. She learns that all the ghosts will be trapped in the house forever unless she's able to determine what lie from the past is keeping them chained to the property. It appeared in 2008 in *Unusual Suspects,* another anthology edited by Dana Stabenow.

In "Chief Executed Officers," there's a series of murders at the office where Lorelai works. To help solve them, she turns to a man she's sworn never to speak to again—her ex-lover, a humanoid alien with highly developed analytical skills. This is a piece I wrote for a serial killer anthology with a science fiction/fantasy edge. The anthology never happened and I haven't had a chance to publish the story anywhere else, so it makes its debut here.

Two of the stories are set in modern day and follow characters coping with recent grief.

In "The Unrhymed Couplets of the Universe," a widower named Henry is suddenly visited by a random collection of everyday objects that briefly materialize and then vanish again. Do they have any connection to his dead wife? The story grew out of a series of conversations I had with two different people on the wildly different topics of email and physics. It appeared in the January 2008 issue of the online magazine *Intergalactic Medicine Show.*

"Can You Hear Me Now?" features a woman named Stacey who is still mourning the loss of her father. But when he begins calling her on her old cell phone, she has to figure out what he wants her to do before his ghost can find peace. It's possible I named the love interest Nathan after one of my favorite actors. The story was written for a 2012 anthology called *The Mammoth Book of Ghost Romance.*

The last two stories are more in the style of classic fantasy, but they too deal with the power of the past to rewrite the present.

In "The Double-Edged Sword," a gifted healer named Aesara has been wandering the land trying to forget a tragedy that happened eleven years ago. She's come to rest in a small town where no one knows her and no one asks her any questions... until one day someone recognizes her and presents her with an impossible task. The story is set in a world I'd created for an unpublished novel, so I already had all the world-building details in my head. I donated it to *Elemental,* a science fiction and fantasy anthology that was published in 2006 as a fundraiser for the tsunami that hit Southeast Asia in 2005. The anthology was edited by Alethea Kontis and Steve Savile. My story was later reprinted in *Year's Best Fantasy* #7, edited by David Hartwell and Kathryn Cramer.

In "Wintermoon Wish," the self-centered Lirril is forced to take stock of her own life when she meets Jake, a young man who is trying to create a future that is more hopeful than his past. The story is set in the world I created for my young adult trilogy: *The Safe-Keeper's Secret, The Truth-Teller's Tale,* and *The Dream-Maker's Magic.* In those books, there is a winter solstice ceremony where everyone burns a wreath decorated with items representing the wishes they hope will come true in the following year. In essence, "Wintermoon Wish" is a Christmas/Yule/New Year's Eve story. (I myself burn a small wreath every year in honor of this celebration.) The story appeared in the 2006 anthology *Firebirds Rising,* edited by Sharyn November.

Enjoy the stories!

# THE SORCERER'S ASSASSIN

When you work at a school for mages, I've learned, it's wise never to leave your room unless you've cloaked yourself in a reflecting spell. That way, as you walk the long, high corridors of arched stone and stained glass, you can feel relatively safe in the knowledge that rancorous or embarrassing spells aimed your way (accidentally or otherwise) will simply bounce off your own enchantment and go sticking onto the perpetrator instead. I can't tell you the number of students I've passed in these halls who have suddenly bloomed into a seven-foot-tall lotus or shrunk to an agitated frog. Yes, of course, I could with little effort reverse any such hex cast on me, but it's so much easier to saunter out into the world knowing I am immune from ill-trained apprentices or maliciously inclined pranksters.

Professor Morben, it was clear, had come to class that morning garbed in no such protection.

I stopped at the doorway of the wide, clean room where he taught Illusions and Transmogrification. Ten or twelve students were huddled against the back wall, wearing their lilac apprentice's robes and looking totally devoid of magic. Professors Dernwerd and Audra were standing over a shape that looked very much like a man who had crumpled to the floor. Dernwerd's thin gray hair was standing up any old which way, as if he had been summoned from the mirror before completing his personal grooming. Audra, of course, looked perfect as always, her dark red hair wound into a tight bun, her gold robes hanging precisely over her sharp, narrow shoulders.

They both looked up at me when I stepped into the room. "He's dead, Camalyn," Dernwerd said in a shaky voice.

I was briefly annoyed. How many times had I told the other teachers to address me as "Headmistress," at least in front of the students? Then the words registered. "Dead?" I repeated. "Morben? Is *dead*? That's not possible!"

Audra looked at me with her cool green eyes. She's only a couple of decades younger than I am, but she looks at least fifty years my junior, and that's only one of the many things I can't stand about her. "Take a look for yourself," she invited. "But I wouldn't advise you to get too close until we've ascertained what happened."

I crossed the room in the stately way I've cultivated and came to a halt a few feet away from the corpse. Yes, there could be no doubt about it. Morben was dead. His face had a riven, petrified look, his mouth gaped in a silent scream, and his eyes gazed up at some unbearable horror. His hands were clenched around his throat as if to choke out his own life or claw at spectral hands bent on that very task. He did not move or breathe or radiate any life heat at all.

I had hated the man, but I had certainly never expected him to come to an end like this. I stared down at him. "What happened to him?"

Dernwerd gestured at the students. "They said he was in the middle of a class on Transmogrification when he suddenly started shrieking and pointing at something on the ceiling. They all looked, of course, but didn't see a thing there. Then he started grabbing at his neck and contorting all around as though someone was squeezing the life out of him. Then he dropped to the floor and he died. In minutes, they said."

I glanced back at the students, a room away but obviously listening to every word. "Is that true?"

They looked at each other and nodded. "Just like he said," confirmed one girl who looked about twelve. I know that magic folk age differently than mortals do, and I'm 105 myself, so everyone looks young to me, but I cannot believe we are now admitting *children* to the school. She was probably eighteen and a very knowing girl, but she looked so young and so innocent that I moved a little to shield her eyes from a view of the body. "He screamed and screamed, until he started choking, then he kept making these terrible little grunting sounds. Like he was trying to tell us something. But we couldn't see anything. We couldn't do anything. It happened so fast."

I looked back at Morben, ghastly and terrified. What could possibly have killed one of the most powerful wizards in the kingdom? Despite Audra's caution to stand clear of the body, I had decided to take a pace closer when the corpse abruptly disintegrated into a smoking pile of black ash. I stepped back hurriedly and brushed some cinder from my sleeve.

"I think we'd better cancel classes for the day," I said, keeping my voice steady to disguise my sudden shakiness. "Time to convene a council of mages."

The Norwitch Academy of Magic and Sorcery had been founded three centuries ago and enjoyed great prestige and prosperity ever since. I was the seventh wizard to ascend to the top position in the school, a feat I had accomplished thirty-eight years before, and the first to preside over an investigation of murder. Not a distinction I particularly wished to claim.

A staff of twenty professors reported to me, and between us we taught a student body of four hundred students. A countless number of cooks, laundresses, gardeners, and stableboys also lived on the premises, making sure life at the school ran smoothly. Thus, in theory, there were close to five hundred suspects in this unsettling murder case.

In actuality, however, the number could be narrowed down to five without any trouble at all. There were, in the entire kingdom, only half a dozen wizards with the knowledge and power to cast a death spell that actually worked. All six of them worked at the Academy, and one was now dead.

The other five of us sat in my office and looked at each other with expressions of mistrust and wonder.

"So!" I said briskly, folding my hands before me on my ornate desk. "I suppose all of you have heard the dreadful news by now. Morben is dead, and someone killed him, and we need to try to discover who and why."

"The why is simple enough," Audra said with some contempt. She sat in one of my stiff high-backed chairs as if it was a comfortably stuffed divan, and her gold robe molded itself to her long legs. Dernwerd, Borrin, and Xander couldn't keep their watery old eyes off her. "He was a foul-mouthed, lecherous, mean-spirited hack, and everybody hated him."

"It's true that he was a difficult man, but you needn't speak so harshly," Dernwerd mumbled in his irritating, apologetic way. As if he thought that even in death Morben might reach out to slap him if he didn't talk nice.

"Yes, but to disapprove of him and to kill him are two very different things," Xander said. Xander was a lean, bald, punctilious scholar who would argue the most minute point of history or spellwork till you wanted to run screaming from the room.

"Frankly, I'm surprised he hasn't been done away with long before now," Borrin drawled. Supercilious, wealthy family background, a north-country accent—Borrin does think he's the most elegant of the wizards, though I'm pretty sure he uses magic to keep his hair silver and his figure trim. I can respect his abilities, which are formidable, but not his vanity.

You will be thinking by now that I dislike almost everyone in my employ, and you would be right. In fact, I am a terrible misanthrope, and my attitude is even worse when it comes to wizards and warlocks. Call me a misosorcerer and be done with it! But I inherited all senior members of my faculty when I joined the school, and I was under contract to keep them. Trust me, otherwise I would have ousted Morben when I first came on board, and I might have fired the other four while I was at it. Though honesty compels me to admit all of them, even Audra, are ferociously talented mages.

And all of them have the ability, if not the inclination, to kill a man by magic.

"Well, he's dead now," I said. "And it seems obvious that one of the five of us murdered him."

They all looked at each other and at me, and none of them said a word.

"The students didn't recognize the spell they described, but I did and I assume you did as well," I went on. "It can be found in the Hazelton *Grimoire*, though a variant without the screaming is indexed in Mortensen's *Spellbook*, and only the five of us have the knowledge to *unlock* either of those volumes, let alone the strength to speak the enchantment. So one of us killed him. Why?"

Dernwerd was on his feet, pointing at Audra. "You're the one who always hated him!" So much for his usual conciliatory manner. "I heard you! Just yesterday in the hall! I heard you tell him that if he touched you again, you'd turn him to ice and iron!"

"And I would have, but he didn't," Audra said furiously. "Aren't you the one he embarrassed in front of his whole class last week when you couldn't recapture the igliat and had to get Morben's help? He said you had the skill of a Rank Five wizard and shouldn't allowed to teach advanced classes."

Dernwerd's face was the same gray color as his hair. "How did you know that?"

She shrugged one thin shoulder. "A couple of the students told me. They thought it was funny."

Borrin was smiling in that detestable way, and Xander gave him a long, thorough look. "You smile now, but you didn't think it was so funny when Morben called you an up-country upstart with imaginary bloodlines," he said in his painstaking way. I had no doubt he had reproduced the quote with shattering accuracy.

Borrin stopped smiling. "My family's older than the kingdom, and if anyone's a sorcerer-come-lately it's Morben with his questionable antecedents and his rough-and-ready magic."

"And, anyway," I said to Xander, "you were none too fond him, either. You were quite public in your hatred for him once he published that paper about the error you made in your *Treatise*."

The bald man glared at me. Borrin was laughing again. "And you, Camalyn?" Borrin said. "Why did you despise the estimable Morben? Because he told the school board that you were a spinster with a poisonous mind and a dried-up heart? Because he told them no female should ever be head of Norwitch Academy, but if they were going to make that mistake, they should at least choose one who could claim to be a *woman*?"

Audra snickered. Dernwerd and Xander looked embarrassed for me. I looked at Borrin and wished him dead. "So one of us killed him." I repeated, "and we all had a reason. Now we have to determine who had the chance. I want each of you to write down a diary where you've been since midnight last night, with names of witnesses who can substantiate your claims. I will begin the investigation."

"What about you?" Borrin said. "You have the skills, and you have the temper. Who will investigate you?"

I pointed at Audra. "Let the *womanly* woman of the group have that privilege," I said coldly. "Though you may all give her whatever assistance you desire. I expect your reports by this afternoon. Now you can go."

All four of them were quick to turn in accounts of their recent activities, and I handed over my own schedule to Audra when she came by my office. I spent a little time reading their reports, but in truth I didn't have much hope that I would learn anything. A good wizard can appear to be in two places at one time; even a bad one can set up a spell in a remote location so that it's triggered by an action or a phrase. How could I possibly check their alibis and prove definitively which one of them was responsible for this crime? Or even—interesting thought—that two or more of them had been involved?

I shut my eyes and leaned back in my well-padded chair, reviewing the case. Well, to be truthful, I had had more reason than any of them to want Morben dead. He had recently gone to the school board to complain about me—my attitude, my abilities, my age—and to suggest himself in the role of headmaster instead. I don't suppose any of them knew that I had managed to audit his entire presentation illicitly. I had planted a magical seashell in the council room and linked its listening ear to another shell set up in my office. It was like being in the room with the rest of them without having to see their stern and self-righteous faces. I found myself disliking the board members as much as I disliked Morben.

But I hadn't included that information in the report I gave Audra.

Which led me to wonder what the others hadn't told me.

Going on pure instinct, I'd have said the likeliest killer was Audra herself. Morben had lusted after her ever since she'd joined academy, and being stalked for more than forty years could wear on the patience of the sweetest woman, which we all knew Audra was not. Moreover, she had always wanted to teach his specialty classes in Illusions and Transmogrification, but he was not about to give them up, so she was stuck with Travel and Time Manipulation, which were useful though much less glamorous skills. Distaste and envy could have combined to make her want to see Morben dead.

The men had fewer incentives, I thought. Dernwerd, in any case, was a whiny and ineffectual man who might smolder with hatred for a hundred years before he brought himself actually to kill someone. Though I'd seen him level a mountain once, with utter grace and precision, so I knew he had more power than his personality might predict.

Xander never seemed to pull his head out of his books long enough to develop any kind of emotional reaction, good or bad, to anyone else alive, so I found it hard to believe he would have nurtured enough animosity to hunt Morben down. Borrin, though. He was smart enough, good enough, and nasty enough to kill a man, and the insult to his family name would probably have been sufficient to send him seeking revenge.

I wrote them all down on a piece of paper, in descending order of probability: *Audra, Borrin, Dernwerd, Xander.* After thinking about it a minute, I squeezed another name between Audra's and Borrin's. *Camalyn.*

That still left Audra as the most likely murderer.

We spent two days canvassing the students and checking Morben's bedchamber and classrooms for any kind of evidence, but found nothing that incriminated anyone. There was no point in suspending school any longer, so we allowed classes to resume the following day. The school board members were all unhappy that the murder was still unsolved, but frantic to resume the educational process so parents didn't start pulling students out. Therefore, none of them made a fuss when we opened the classrooms again.

All was relatively serene for a week, and I began to grow a little more cheerful about the whole thing: *Well, Morben's dead, and we have a murderer in our midst, but that killer has done us all a favor, really, so maybe we should just let the whole thing go and get on with our lives.* Unrealistic, you'll say. Absolutely, I'll agree.

About ten days after Morben's death I was heading down the hall between my Alchemy class and my Protective Spells seminar when I heard a sound of hysterical shrieking. Of course, I ran in that direction, as did the other five hundred people on the school property. I noted that Audra came puffing up from the southern stairway, and that Dernwerd and Xander arrived at the same time, as if they had been consulting together when the cries were raised.

The commotion was coming from Borrin's Animal Languages classroom. We rushed inside as if by hurrying we could affect the outcome of events that had already been put in motion. Naturally, we could not.

The scene greatly resembled the one from ten days earlier. Students cowered against the back wall of the room and a wizard lay dead on the floor, face contorted in horror, hands clamped around his own throat. But this time I was not about to let myself be thwarted by the spell. I muttered a command of my own, and the body remained intact. No smoking pile of ashes. Gruesome though it was, we would be able to examine the corpse for evidence.

The other three wizards had come to stand beside me and were staring down at Borrin with many emotions on their faces, none of them grief. They were angry, and they were afraid, for what can kill two wizards can kill three, or six. I raised my voice to address the students. "Clear the room, please," I said. "The professors and I must talk."

As soon as the door had closed behind them, the accusations started.

"You!" Dernwerd screeched, pointing at Audra. "You did this! I was with Xander all morning, I know he and I are innocent, but where were you before you came running up to investigate the alarm?"

"I was in the archives with many junior professors nearby," she said icily. "I did not speak to any of them, but I'm sure one or two will remember seeing me there. And as for the two of you being guilt-free—who's to say you didn't execute this little scheme together? I would think that would be a nice, convenient way to operate."

Dernwerd boggled at her. Xander shook his bald head. "And who's to say it's only the three of us who might have engineered this death?" he asked quietly. "For who saw Camalyn before she arrived on the scene? Where had she been earlier in the morning?"

"Yes, Camalyn!" Dernwerd exclaimed. "Explain your actions, please!"

"I would be much more likely to dismiss you than kill you if I wanted to see any of you gone from here," I said in a hard voice. "But it is very clear that we now have a murderer in our midst who is working his or her way through the senior staff. One of the four of us. Trust me, I want to identify and destroy this person, but my first priority is safety— for the students at this school and the master wizards who remain alive."

"And what do you propose?" Audra sneered. "That the four of us stay always in sight of each other, watching and waiting? A bad idea, I think! Whoever has the strength to kill us one by one might easily have the ability to kill three of us at once. We should at least scatter throughout the halls and make his life more difficult."

Xander gave her a searching look. "So—you would rather be unobserved, Audra, would you?" he asked slowly. "What actions are you hiding? Why so secretive?"

"Why so trusting?" she shot back. "Perhaps I feel I have a better chance to protect myself if you three bumblers aren't nearby to hamper me."

"For the moment, I see no practical way for us to shadow each other day and night," I said, mostly just to stop the bickering. "Those of you who wish to keep a fellow company may do so. If you want to spy on each other," I added with some malice, "I will not stop you from doing that, either. I will examine the body and see what evidence it might yield."

"Oh, no, you will not!" Audra exclaimed. "I will stand here and watch every threadbare clue you lift from Borrin's corpse, or every false clue you plant there when you think none of us are looking."

Xander and Dernwerd exchanged uneasy glances. "Yes—she's right—I think we had better stay too," Dernwerd said apologetically. "In case one of us notices something another one overlooks—"

"Fine. Stay. And help," I snapped. "Let us get this autopsy under way."

But we found nothing helpful except the glimmer of magic. And even it bore no signature we could trace. Eventually I summoned the gardeners and told them they were turned gravediggers. Borrin would be buried beside the trellis of calysian roses that bloomed through all seasons. A better end than he deserved, actually, but it did not seem to be the time to be raking up past differences.

None of us heard from our murderer again for three more days. Again, I had permitted classes to resume, though everyone crept through the hallway with a sort of hunched and hunted gait, as if expecting at any moment horror would incorporate out of the very air. I was fairly certain the students and the staff had no reason to worry but I was just as sure our renegade would eventually strike again at one of the senior wizards.

I was right. The killer came for me.

I had stepped outside for a breath of winter air and was walking along the lovely stone promenade that was attached to the second story of the school and overlooked the gardens. Little to see in the gardens at that season but hardy evergreens and hopeful brown stalks that, in a few months, would be animated by an even more ancient and powerful magic than mine. I always loved gardens in winter. They made me believe that even old and ugly and withered creatures possessed the potential for beauty and rebirth.

I had completed my first pass down the promenade and was just pivoting to make the return trip when I felt the unmistakable frisson of sorcery skitter across my skin. I paused, one foot on the floor, one foot lifted to step.

All around me, unfolding and refolding in infinite permutations, I saw reflections of myself caught in the exact same pose. I knew instantly what had happened, of course. Someone had cast a multiplying curse on me, assuming that I would never have gone out in the world unprotected, but also assuming that I had arrayed myself in a different kind of enchantment altogether. For instance, it might be supposed that I had summoned an artillery spell that was designed to fire off damaging shots as soon as it was activated by someone else's magic. A multiplying curse goes on and on and on without end—I would have been igniting so many deadly explosions that within minutes I would have died in my own detonations.

Never had my assailant expected that I would have kept my simple old reflecting spell in place. So this replicating curse, while impossibly annoying, was completely harmless. All it did was show thousands of copies of me, millions, putting down my foot and looking around, trying to gaze through my own reflections to determine who had accosted me.

I admit I was not surprised when I was finally able to make out Audra standing on the promenade before me, her eyes closed, her lips moving, as she quickly invoked a different bit of magic. I moved rapidly myself, tossing up a wall of protection that should be able to frustrate even the most virulent curse, for a while at least. Then, through my own still, watchful horde of sentries, I peered at her, trying to guess what she might do next.

She was gesturing more forcefully. Her red hair was unbound and whipping in an ensorcelled wind, and her gold robes clung to a body that was more voluptuous than I remembered it being. I had always believed Audra to be constructed of bones, spite, and magic, but clearly dislike had colored my perceptions.

Or desire had colored someone else's.

I looked more closely. Last time I had seen her, Audra's hair had not been quite so luxuriant, nor so long. Nor was she usually this tall, and her angular face was far from being beautiful in the normal run of things. And, may I say, I am not in the habit of rating other women's physical attractions, but in my opinion, she generally had none. At the moment, her bosom was very well endowed.

This was not Audra. This was someone's idealization of Audra.

I knew of only one truly gifted illusionist who had also been in love with the red-haired witch. Apparently Morben was not dead after all. We had never had a chance to inspect his body, I suddenly remembered. We had assumed that the original death spell was what had caused the corpse to flare to ashes, but that had just been part and parcel of the overall illusion. There had been no body to examine because there was no body. Morben had projected the whole scene of assault and death, then caused the final image to vanish with a flick of his fingers. How could we have been so stupid?

I had just been so happy he was dead.

But if I didn't show some ingenuity immediately, I would be the one dead, and Morben would be the one who was happy. I could feel him testing my wall of protection, flinging first one angry spell and then another against my magical shield. He was very good at mayhem; he would be able to find a way through it eventually. And then every single copy of Camalyn the Headmistress would fall to the stone floor, choking on death and fury.

I considered the situation, tilting my head to one side. All my reflections did likewise. I was maintaining two simultaneous sets of magic, the reflecting spell and the spell of protection. Morben, meanwhile, juggled two of his own, the illusion of Audra and the attack on me. That level of magical use had probably drained both of us to an approximately equal level.

But if I could reduce my expenditure of energy to one spell only, I should be stronger than my enemy. I would have to work very fast, of course. I would have to know exactly what I was doing before I made a single move.

Morben's curses hammered at my shield. I concentrated on holding the wall in place while conjuring and dispersing other bits of magic. My mirrored images all raised their hands before them, as if to plead for mercy or feel for an unseen door. I murmured a word, and all my doppelgangers fell away.

The counterfeit Audra whipped around to face me, her beautiful mouth stretched into a disdainful smile. "One of you or a thousand of you, it does not matter," Morben said in Audra's voice. "I will slay you all."

I had never gotten much pleasure out of bandying words with Morben, and I did not bother now. I merely extended my right hand and spoke a single word. "*Stone.*"

The other wizard turned to a statue with its mouth half-open and its hands lifted as if to strike. He did not move again.

I stood there a moment, smiling, then resumed my habitual reflecting spell. You could never tell where the next danger might come from, or when. It was not possible to be too careful.

To tell the truth, I had expected a more emotional reaction from the school board and my fellow wizards once it was discovered who the killer was and how I had vanquished him. Something along the lines of, "Oh, Camalyn, you're so wise, we're so grateful, you've saved us all" would have been entirely appropriate, I thought. Instead, the head of the school board merely said, "I suppose you'll be wanting funds to hire some new instructors." My remaining staff quarreled amongst themselves over who had been most delinquent in overlooking the obvious clues that pointed to the notion that Morben was not really dead.

I was not surprised when they ultimately decided I was most to blame. "Had Camalyn figured this out sooner," Xander said, "Borrin would not be dead."

I could not be entirely sorry that my deductions had been so slow.

The corollary event that probably made me happiest about the whole affair was how angry Audra was that the cautionary statuary on the promenade looked just like her, with a few enhancements.

"You could have turned him back into *Morben* before you turned him into stone forever," she said a few days after the incident was concluded.

"I could have, if I had wanted to risk dying for your vanity," I agreed. "I only had time for one spell. I chose to incapacitate him, not de-beautify him."

"What if he breaks free of enchantment?" Dernwerd asked in a fretful voice. "What if he comes back to life and kills us all?"

I shrugged. I wasn't too worried about it. A wizard's spell generally will last for that wizard's lifetime, so I, at least, should be dead before Morben had any reasonable chance of resurrection. "Get out the sledgehammer and shatter him to bits," I said. "Grind him into dust and let the wind blow him away. It's all the same to me."

"But are we just to leave him like that forever?" Xander asked. "It seems so indecent, somehow. What kind of lesson does that present for the students?"

"Not to try to kill the Headmistress," I said over my shoulder, for I was bored with the conversation and already walking away. "I don't know that they need to learn anything else while they're here at Norwitch."

And, come to think of it, I'm not sure any of them did.

# In the House of
# Seven Spirits

I had thought it would bother me to live in a haunted house, but in fact I grew fond of the ghosts in an amazingly short time.

The agent from whom I rented the property for the summer had been very clear about the amenities—three bedrooms, two bathrooms, renovated kitchen, wi-fi DSL, cable TV, a small back yard, weekly yard service, and seven unevictable tenants.

"Some people never see them," he told me, his dark eyes earnest and his pale face severe. He'd tried to talk me out of renting the place, but I couldn't pass up its dirt-cheap price. Writers just don't make that much money, and I had almost despaired of finding someplace I could afford for a few months while I put my life back together. "But everyone always reports a sense of being watched. Accompanied. I don't believe they'll harm you. But you might be—uncomfortable."

*Uncomfortable* was staying in the tiny New York apartment with Steve while we hammered out the terms of a divorce. Could seven sad wraiths fill me with as much anger and despair? Hard to believe.

"How did they die?" I asked.

He reeled them off as if he'd given this particular speech too often to count. "Martin shot his wife, Suzanne, and her lover, Bradley, when he came home and found them together. Then he killed himself. That was fifteen years ago. A couple years after that, two elderly women, Victoria and Charlotte, died of carbon monoxide poisoning—that's been taken care of, by the way. A middle-aged man named Edison fell down the stairs and broke his neck. Lizzie died of spinal meningitis when she was nine years old. Her mother thought she just had a bad case of the flu. That was three years ago. No one's died in the house since because no one's lived there very long."

"Who owns the place?"

"Family members. I deal most often with a niece who owns and rents out a number of properties in the area." He gave me another serious look. "You should think hard before you decide you want to live in this house."

"I'll chance it. I ain't afraid of no ghosts."

He didn't laugh. Maybe he didn't get the reference. I wrote out a check for my first month's rent, got a map, got a key, and set out for my new home.

I was met just inside the front door by an older woman with curly gray hair and a wide, hopeful smile. I'd always thought ghosts would be a misty white, floating from room to room like errant wisps of smoke. But this one was colorful in a pink-and-purple patterned blouse and navy blue trousers. Insubstantial, though—she looked like a watercolor painted on a sheet of gauze. I could see straight through her to the polished taupe of the walls.

Despite the rental agent's warning, I was startled to see her, and I dropped my key. "Hello!" I said, feeling my heart beat suddenly harder. "Um—I'm the new tenant. Erica. I'm here for the summer. Hope that's all right."

She clapped her hands together, though they made no sound, and looked delighted. "You can *see* me!" she exclaimed. "Oh, I'm so glad. The couple who were here last—well—they clearly knew when one of us was in the room, but no matter how loud we were or how much we waved our arms, they just never seemed to be able to *focus*. They didn't stay long," she added sadly. "We didn't mean to frighten them. I hope you won't be afraid."

Indeed, my heart had already settled down to a normal pace. She looked like somebody's grandmother, just in from the kitchen after having made a batch of cookies. "Not afraid yet," I said. "Which one are you?"

She smiled again. "Victoria. So pleased to meet you."

I glanced around. "Maybe you can give me a tour of the house."

It was a lovely place, probably eighty years old, two stories of hardwood floors and hard plaster walls and shabby chic furniture that someone had picked out with care. But my first walk-through was a little—unusual.

"Here's the kitchen, where Martin died," Victoria said, showing me the small but spotless black-and-white tiled room. The dining room hadn't seen much action, but the living room was the place where "Charlotte and I were watching TV when we were overcome by carbon monoxide poisoning." She sighed. "We only got to see the first couple seasons of *The X-Files*. I always wanted to know what happened."

"There were a couple of movies, too," I said.

"I know! Never got to see them, either."

So they must have died before 1998. "Were you and Charlotte sisters?"

"Lifelong friends. Widows. We moved in together after her husband died." She headed toward the stairs, gesturing at a pretty rug placed beneath the very bottom step. "That's where Edison lay dying after he fell and broke his neck. He was alive for quite some time, but none of us could figure out how to use the phone and call for help. Very tragic."

I stepped gingerly on the floral pattern of the rug. "He just fell?"

She glanced over her shoulder at me, an impish look in her eye. "Well. He *says* that Martin pushed him. Impossible, of course. Martin *may* have appeared suddenly and frightened him, causing him to take a misstep, but he doesn't have any more strength than the rest of us."

I swallowed. Martin was the only one of the ghosts who had violence associated with his past, at least as far as I knew. "Would he—is Martin the kind of person who would *want* to shove someone down the stairs? Did he frighten Edison on purpose?"

"Martin *is* very angry," Victoria admitted. "It's my theory that no one who dies in this house will ever be permitted to leave as long as Martin's spirit is still tethered here. But did he try to kill Edison? I doubt it. He dislikes Edison even more than the rest of us do. I wouldn't think Martin would have wanted to be stuck with him for—well, forever."

I thought that over as Victoria showed me through the upstairs rooms. "Here's the bedroom where Bradley and Suzanne were killed. Some people say you can still see the blood on the floor, but *I've* never been able to make it out... This is the bedroom where Lizzie died. Poor thing. She was so *hot*. Charlotte and I stayed with her all night because, you know, a ghost can bring a chill to the air and we hoped it would bring her fever down. But no such luck. Her body went still and then her spirit just sat up. She looked at us and said, 'I guess I'm here with you two now.'"

Lizzie's room was smaller, for Bradley and Suzanne had been killed in the master bedroom, but I liked it better. More light streamed in through the two tall windows, and the view showed the small green backyard. And, OK, I was less unnerved by the idea of sleeping alongside the ghost of a girl who had died of illness than the thought of sharing a bed with the spirits of two murder victims.

"I think I'll make this my bedroom," I said.

Victoria gestured down the hall. "The third bedroom is quite nice, and no one died there," she said. Clearly I hadn't fooled her at all.

So I followed her into a room about the size of Lizzie's, and prettily furnished, but it was instantly clear to me that this would be my last choice. For one thing, the sun had a hard time making its way through the single side window. For another, the room was significantly colder than any other room in the house.

For another, it really was haunted.

A thin, bony-faced woman sat on the bed, apparently reciting a story to a small blonde girl who leaned against her, smiling sleepily. They had to be Charlotte and Lizzie. A dark-haired young woman stood at the window, looking out; I could only see her profile, but the twist of her mouth was bitter and dissatisfied. A few feet away from her stood a short, pudgy man who looked like he had once been ruddy and choleric. He was talking so loudly that I couldn't hear the tale Charlotte was spinning for Lizzie.

"If you'd only *ask* him to be more thoughtful. He'll listen to *you*. But, no, you're too selfish to think about anyone but yourself or anything but your own misery."

The woman at the window ignored him, but Charlotte gave him an icy stare. "For God's sake, Edison, no one has ever had any success at getting Martin to behave in any but the most abominable fashion, and your incessant complaining is about to drive every single one of us stark raving mad. Will you just *shut up?*"

I couldn't help it. I laughed. Instantly, they were all staring at me. I had the strange sensation that *they* hadn't seen *me* when I walked through the door—as if whatever plane ghosts existed on really didn't intersect with the ordinary world, at least all the time. I tried to smooth away my smile. "Sorry," I said. "I'm Erica. Victoria's showing me around."

Charlotte looked at Victoria with her eyebrows raised. "She sees *all* of us?"

"I see you and the little girl—Lizzie?—and Edison," I volunteered. "And someone at the window. Suzanne, I guess. I haven't seen Martin or—" For a moment I blanked on his name. "Or Bradley yet." I glanced at Victoria. "Did I miss them?"

She shook her head. "They must be in the yard. They can't go past the property boundaries, but both of them like to be outside of the house."

Charlotte stood up, urging Lizzie forward. I had the feeling that the older woman would have offered me her hand, except long experience had taught her it was a hard trick for a ghost. "How very nice to meet you," she said, her voice more reserved than Victoria's but her pleasure just as genuine. "We hope you'll enjoy your stay."

Lizzie jumped up and down. "Will you play with me? Will you read me stories? Charlotte tells me stories all the time, but she doesn't know any new ones. Will you go to the library and check out new books for me? And read them to me? Every night?"

I was charmed. "I will. What kinds of books do you like?"

Edison made a huffing sound. "Oh, sure, the cute little girl gets all the attention! It doesn't matter what anyone else wants. You could read *me* Tom Clancy books, but will you? I don't think so!"

"Shut up, Edison," Suzanne said. She had moved away from the window and was heading for the door. It seemed to me that she had less color than all the others—she was a closer approximation of my idea of a ghost—that her very manner and expression were drenched in sadness. She gave me one unfathomable look and slipped out the door.

"Well, nobody cares about me," Edison muttered. "I'm the one everyone always forgets."

"I don't think I'll forget you, Edison," I said cheerfully. "I think we'll all be friends."

And oddly, we were. I mean, almost right away. As soon as I hauled all my stuff in from the car, I headed out to run errands. I picked up food at the grocery store, books at the library, and DVDs at Blockbuster. That very night, I set up entertainment zones in four separate rooms of the house. I'd rented a few seasons of *The X-Files* for Charlotte and Victoria, and I set up the first discs to play in the living room. Victoria told me that Bradley liked PBS shows, so I had the little TV in the kitchen tuned to the local public television station, even though Bradley still hadn't made an appearance. For Edison, I'd rented a selection of Dean Koontz, Stephen King, and Tom Clancy books on CD, and I had one of these running on my laptop up in the third bedroom where the ghosts seemed to like to congregate.

Lizzie and I settled into her room/my room and I read her half of a *Baby-Sitter's Club* book. She leaned against me just as she had against Charlotte, listening happily. There was no weight to her body, but I felt a coolness against my skin, as if a curl of winter had blown through the window and come to rest companionably at my side.

Victoria had said there was no way to make Martin happy, so I didn't bother trying to figure out what I might do for him. The rest of us passed a very enjoyable evening, and I could feel the contentment radiating throughout the entire house. Indeed, when I finally turned out the light and went to bed, I fell asleep almost instantly and I didn't wake 'til dawn.

My first night in the haunted house was far more peaceful than my last hundred nights in the apartment I shared with my husband. Had my life held so many terrors lately that I had actually *upgraded* it by moving in with restless spirits? Had the world of the living proved so perilous that I was more at ease among the dead?

The following weeks quickly settled into a pattern. During the day, I worked on my novel, occasionally taking breaks to walk around the neighborhood, explore the town, or replenish supplies. In the evenings, I hung out with my new roommates. Now and then I was able to find a movie or program that everyone in the household could agree on— *Buffy* was a universal favorite, for instance, and even Edison enjoyed Pixar movies—but most of the time I activated the distinct entertainment zones that everyone preferred. Edison developed the habit of heading down to the kitchen to watch PBS with Bradley once the CD of the day had finished playing. I knew that, because he also developed the annoying habit of telling the rest of us the next day what he'd learned the night before about Mayan ruins or asteroid belts or creatures of the deep sea. This was preferable to his other favorite topic of conversation, however, which was to claim that Martin had murdered him by pushing him down the stairs.

I didn't know what Bradley thought about sharing his TV viewing time with Edison. During those first two weeks, neither Bradley nor Martin made an appearance. I couldn't decide if I should be sorry or glad.

I did meet a few of my neighbors, though. The young couple on the right usually just waved as they left for work in the mornings, and the older woman on my left never wanted to talk about anything but how late the paperboy was, but the woman who lived behind me was gregarious and cheerful. A low tangle of honeysuckle divided our yards and perfumed our conversations as we stood on either side to talk.

That first day, she introduced herself as Janet and waved at me with a trowel. She was a fiftyish brown-haired woman dressed in shapeless gardening clothes and a big straw hat that partially obscured her face. "You're the new renter?" she asked. "How are you getting along with the ghosts?"

She said it in a playful way that made me think she was joking. So I gave a noncommittal answer and a big smile. "Very well, thank you. They don't trouble me at all."

She laughed. "Excellent! So perhaps you'll stay longer than the last few tenants. I think one of them decamped within a week."

"I'd like to stay," I admitted. "I'm falling in love with the house." I fanned myself with the magazine I'd been reading on the back porch before I spotted Janet. "How long have you lived here?"

"Oh, let's see—goodness, I think I moved in twenty years ago."

"So you must have been living here when the murders happened," I said.

She nodded. "It was terrible. I was very close to Suzanne. I kept telling her to leave Martin. He was so unstable, it was so *obvious* he would turn violent if he ever found out about Bradley. I'd had an abusive husband of my own, and so I knew—" Janet paused and shook her head. "But she wouldn't listen to me. And when that sweet girl was murdered, I wept for days."

"Were you here when it happened?"

She nodded. "I saw the police cars and I ran over to see if I could help. I'm a nurse at the ER and—but they were all long dead."

I thought she might be weeping now, all these years later, and I hastily changed the subject. "My other neighbors seem very nice," I said. "I haven't had very long conversations with them, though."

"Oh, I like them all," she said. "But I think Joan and Bruce might be moving soon. She wants a dog."

"And? She can't have a dog here?"

Janet shook her head. "It's your house. Animals don't like it. Last three or four times one of the near neighbors has tried to get a dog—any dog—the animal would just refuse to calm down. Would stand right there in the yard, facing your house, and bark its head off. Cats won't stay either. They run off the first time they can get out the door."

I was disappointed. I'd been thinking about getting a cat. "Maybe the house really *is* haunted," I said softly.

Janet smiled sadly. "Oh, I'm convinced it is."

I was working on my book one afternoon when a ghost I hadn't seen before stalked in and settled in the chair across from my desk. "I suppose you're not going to leave," he said in a dark voice.

He startled me. I believe an undignified "eek!" actually passed my lips, but I wasn't exactly afraid. I saved my file and closed my laptop so I could study him. A handsome man, I decided. I guessed Suzanne to be about thirty, and this man was maybe a year or two older. He had rumpled brown hair and an intense gaze that gave him a brooding air. Altogether, he cultivated a somewhat Byronic manner that suited my notions of ghosthood as much as Suzanne's die-away despair. "Which one are you?" I inquired.

He sneered. "You mean, am I the wronged husband or the doomed lover? The murderer or the fool?"

"Yes," I said calmly. "That's what I meant."

He didn't answer for a moment. I made sure to take in details of his face and clothing so that I could ask Victoria later whom I had had the pleasure of meeting, in case he never told me. But he shrugged and said, "I'm the fool."

I propped my chin on my hand. "For loving a married woman?" I said. "Lot of people make that mistake."

He snorted. "For believing she was worth loving."

My eyebrows rose. This was a new twist. "You and Suzanne had a falling out? Was this the night you were—were discovered?"

He looked away. "No. That night I loved her as much as I ever had. It was just—later—when I found out—" He shook his head. "How could I ever have loved someone like her?" he burst out.

My eyes went wide. "You discovered something—after you died? A secret about Suzanne?"

He watched me a moment with those dark eyes. Sexy. *Just a little more corporeal mass,* I found myself thinking, *and*

*I'd want to sleep with you, too.* "Doesn't everyone have secrets?" he asked at last. "Don't you?"

I reviewed my own life. "Things I don't like to talk about, maybe," I allowed. "Not necessarily secrets."

"I have to wonder about someone who seems to be perfectly happy when she's living in a house that harbors seven ghosts and the memories of three murders."

"Three? Oh, you mean Edison?" I said, a little amused. "I haven't encountered Martin yet, but did he really push Edison down the steps?"

Bradley was sneering. Still attractive. "He talked about wanting to do it almost from the day the man moved in."

I almost laughed. "I'm sure the rest of you tried to dissuade him. To be stuck with Edison forever!"

Bradley didn't smile. Indeed, his gaze became even more intense as he hitched himself forward on the chair. "You must help me," he said. "Help all of us. We're trapped in this house together—for time everlasting—hating each other, unable to get away. For so long I wanted Martin dead, but once he died—he's the one who keeps us all here. Put him at rest, and all of us will be at peace."

"But how do I do that?" I asked, bewildered.

Bradley stood up. "Uncover the lie," he said. "Once a living person knows the truth, we will all be free." And, before my eyes, he vanished.

"I don't know what truth he means," Victoria said. She was helping me make dinner that night. I wasn't much of a cook, and of course Victoria couldn't eat, but apparently she'd been something of a chef in her day. We had gotten in the habit of meeting in the kitchen a couple nights a week so she could walk me through one of her favorite recipes. "The truth is that Martin killed Bradley and Suzanne, then killed himself. No, dear, not *that* much garlic."

"But maybe that's *not* the truth," I said. "Maybe Suzanne is really the one who shot Bradley and herself. Maybe that's what Bradley meant. And Martin's been blamed all this time. Maybe that's why he's so mad. I'd be mad, too."

"She was shot in the back, so I don't think so," Victoria said. "But, you know, ever since I've been here, there's been some trouble between Bradley and Suzanne. You would think that lovers who had been murdered together would cling to each other in the afterlife, but that's never been the case. They're almost never in the same room, and if Suzanne comes in the kitchen while Brad is here, he simply walks out. You can tell that she's devastated, after all this time. She doesn't know why he no longer loves her. Because she loves him still."

I tasted the sauce I was creating for my pasta del mar. Victoria was right. Not *that* much garlic. "Is that why she seems so sad? I mean, even for a ghost, she seems—miserable. Inconsolable." I smiled at Victoria. "*You* seem quite happy."

"Well, I always was," she said comfortably. "No need to change now."

Edison wandered through and made a great show of holding his nose. "I hate the smell of fish. Makes me want to vomit."

"Shut up, Edison," Victoria said, and he *humphed* and stalked out.

Edison had also complained a couple nights ago when I ate some takeout crab rangoon. "I don't know, maybe I shouldn't eat seafood while I'm living here," I said with a sigh. "I hate for him to be offended."

Victoria was unimpressed. "If you're going to worry about all of *our* food preferences, you won't be able to eat a thing," she said. "Suzanne is a vegetarian, Lizzie hates broccoli, Bradley is allergic to tomatoes and blueberries, red wine gives Charlotte a migraine, and Martin is lactose intolerant."

"What about you?"

Victoria smiled. "I eat everything." She looked suddenly wistful. "Or I used to. Now, of course, I can't taste a thing."

"I still wonder what Bradley meant," I said. "I did a Google search about the murder—"

"A what?" Victoria repeated.

"Google. It's—it helps you find information on the internet." She still looked mystified, so I shook my head. "Never mind. I think I'll have to go to the library and see if they have microfiche with newspaper coverage. Maybe that will give me some ideas."

"Oh, I have a scrapbook," Victoria said. "After we moved in, I looked up the stories about Brad and Suzanne and Martin. There wasn't much," she added. "It was such a very common and obvious crime."

After my meal (which was pretty good, if heavy on seasoning), Victoria led me to the living room, where a jumble of books and old magazines filled two built-in bookcases.

"All your stuff is still here?" I asked. "That's convenient."

Victoria nodded and settled on the floor to scan the bottom shelf. It was completely filled with scrapbooks and photo albums. A treasure trove for me to look through on some future date, I decided. She said, "We were only renting the house from Suzanne's sister, but we planned to live here a good long time. She let us decorate however we wished—and then she just kept everything in the house so she could rent it out furnished. I think she knew right then she would never have boarders who stayed very long. There, I think that's the book you want."

I pulled out the volume she indicated and began leafing through the pages. This wasn't one of those modern scrapbooks with decorative papers and fancy borders. No, it was just a couple of sturdy covers wrapped around thick black pages. In it, Victoria had collected all sorts of news clippings related to events in this decade of her life—her husband's death, her son's Army heroics, her granddaughter's baptism.

Articles about the murder/suicide appeared late in the book, and I sat right there on the floor and read them. The first thing I found out was that Martin hadn't killed himself with a gun, as I'd always believed.

"He took morphine?" I said, looking up from the page to stare at Victoria. "He shot two people, but he couldn't stand to shoot himself?"

"It's harder to bear pain than it is to inflict it," Victoria said.

The second thing I learned was that Martin really was cold-blooded. Police theorized that Martin had come home unexpectedly, heard voices, retrieved his gun from the living room case where he always kept it, crept upstairs, and shot his wife and her lover. Then he'd come back downstairs, laid the gun on the kitchen table, opened a beer, eaten a bowl of leftover chili, and turned on the football game. (The television was still playing the next day when police came to investigate why his wife wasn't at work.) He appeared to have chased his second beer with a handful of morphine tablets, which took effect when he was back in the kitchen (looking for his third beer, they believed).

"Where'd he get the morphine?" I asked Victoria. "It doesn't say."

She pointed at the book. "Next article."

I turned the page and read another story that gave more detail about the troubled couple. A friend was speculating that their marriage had started to show signs of strain the year before, when his mother moved into their house as she was dying of cancer. "Probably some leftover morphine in the medicine cabinet," Victoria said. "Surely his mother had a prescription."

I nodded. "Makes sense. Still. This is even creepier than before."

"Now you know why the rest of us are just as happy when Martin keeps to himself."

But Martin made an unexpected, and not particularly welcome, appearance just the next day. I had gone to the third bedroom—the place I was most likely to find ghosts—and had been lucky enough to discover Suzanne alone. As usual, she stood at the single window, looking insubstantial enough to evaporate, but weighted in place by the heaviness of grief.

"I want to ask you some questions," I said, speaking fast. Suzanne never hung around for long, so it was best to skip any amenities and get straight to the point. "When you were married—why didn't you leave Martin?"

She didn't turn around to look at me. "I was afraid of him. I thought he'd kill me." She gave a small laugh. "And he did."

"Did Brad want you to run away with him?"

"Yes. Said we could change our names. Move to a different state. Move to a different country. Said he would always love me." She sniffed, as if holding back tears.

"But Brad is angry at you now. Why?"

She didn't answer for a moment. "He won't tell me," she said at last. "He just says I'm not worth loving anymore."

Well, *that* was unhelpful. "Do you have a guess?"

Even if she'd planned to answer, she didn't get a chance. "Don't ask a lying *bitch* for information!" a voice roared, and I jumped nearly a foot in the air. The room was suddenly ice cold and dark with shadows. I could just make out a lumbering shape—big body, small head, fisted hands—an even more insubstantial spirit than Suzanne. "Goddamn *whore* would say anything she thought you would believe!"

Suzanne choked down a cry and hurried past him, out of the room. I didn't know if I should be glad for her or worried for myself that Martin didn't follow. Instead, he stayed facing me, panting heavily, swinging his little head from side to side. I wrapped my arms around myself and wished I had a sweater.

"I suppose you're Martin," I said.

"Get the hell out of my house!" he bellowed.

I stood my ground. "I'm just trying to help," I said calmly. "I want to understand what happened that night."

"What happened? What *happened?* I found my wife screwing another man, that's what happened! Should have strangled both of them with my bare hands. Bitch deserved to die staring me right in the face."

"Why didn't you shoot yourself?" I asked.

He took three quick steps closer and I felt myself enveloped in menace and chill. Suddenly I believed Edison when he said Martin had deliberately forced him down the stairs. I was pretty sure Martin would like to shove me out the window. "Because I didn't want to give her the satisfaction," he spat. "Why don't *you* shoot yourself?"

Shooting, no; running, yes. I was shivering, and frightened, and trying to edge past him toward the door, when suddenly I felt a flurry in the air behind him. "Martin!" came Charlotte's stern voice. "You leave her alone *right this minute.* Such behavior! Out of the room—out, I say!"

He turned on her with a curse, but Bradley and Edison flanked her on either side. I wondered wildly whether ghosts could touch each other, even if they couldn't touch living people, and if that meant the other three could manhandle Martin out the door. But they didn't need to. He snarled something unintelligible at the three of them and stomped into the hall. Instantly, the room warmed by fifteen degrees.

"My heroes," I said faintly. "Thanks, guys."

That night I rented season two of *Buffy* and all of us, minus Martin, gathered in the living room to watch. I worried that the storyline might be a little violent at times for Lizzie, but she just curled up on Charlotte's lap and covered her eyes any time there was too much blood. Suzanne and Bradley were both in the room, though in opposite corners, and her eyes were on him more often than they were on the screen. For the most part, he ignored her, but if ghosts could be said to have body language, I was sure he was highly aware of her.

What had gone wrong between the lovers?

After the first DVD, I was too tired to stay awake any longer. "Want me to set up the next disc or just turn the channel to TCM?" I asked through a yawn.

"TCM," Victoria and Charlotte said in unison. Victoria added, "There's a Barbara Stanwyck retrospective. I just love her movies."

"Then movies you shall have," I said, and flipped the necessary switches. *Double Indemnity* had already started before I was halfway up the stairs.

I woke at noon the next day and sat straight up in bed. Maybe if I'd stayed up to watch the movie, the revelation would have hit me the night before. It was certainly the stuff of cinema: Woman schemes to kill her husband, ensnaring an innocent man in her plan. Except Bradley hadn't had any idea what Suzanne planned to do. Easy enough for her to crush a few morphine tablets and slip them into a container of leftover chili, then wait for Martin to come home and make himself dinner. All she had to do was not eat the doctored food.

I frowned and leaned back against the headboard. But unless she'd told Bradley not to eat the chili, how could she be sure *he* wouldn't accidentally take the drugs? And it was clear Bradley had had no idea Suzanne intended to do away with her husband. Once he'd found out, he was horrified. But how to warn him off without giving herself away?

I heard Victoria's voice in my head. *Suzanne is a vegetarian, Lizzie hates broccoli, Bradley is allergic to tomatoes and blueberries, red wine gives Charlotte a migraine, and Martin is lactose intolerant.*

Safe to leave poisoned chili in the fridge for Martin. The allergy-stricken Brad would never eat it.

I drew up my knees and thought hard. So. Martin hadn't killed himself after all. He came home, shot his wife and her lover, and *didn't* shoot himself because he didn't *plan* to kill himself. *I wouldn't give her the satisfaction.* Still, it didn't make it any less creepy that he'd gone back downstairs, opened a beer, microwaved the chili, and settled in to watch the game while Suzanne and Bradley lay dead upstairs.

I frowned again. Unless that hadn't been exactly how the story played out…

I jumped up, threw on some clothes, paused long enough to brush my teeth, and began hunting for Suzanne. She wasn't in the third bedroom with Charlotte and Lizzie, nor on the stairwell landing with Edison.

"Martin pushed me down the steps, you know," he said in his whiny voice as I hurried past.

"Shut up, Edison," I said automatically and bounded down the stairs. Suzanne wasn't in the living room with Bradley (TCM was still on, playing John Wayne movies now), and she wasn't in the kitchen with Victoria.

"Garden," Victoria said when I asked. "Why? Erica, you look so excited!"

"I think I've solved it," I said.

I heard Brad's voice behind me. He must have noticed my wild-eyed look, too, and followed me into the kitchen. "Solved what?" he asked.

I shook my head and pushed through the back door. Suzanne was sitting on a little bench set near the house, facing Janet's back yard. There was a woman working in the garden, but I didn't think it was Janet. At any rate, she didn't straighten up and wave, as Janet always did.

"Suzanne," I said as I strode toward the bench, trailed by Victoria and Bradley. "*You* did it. *You* killed Martin."

I heard Victoria's gasp and Bradley's little hiss of victory, but Suzanne jumped to her feet. "I did *not!*" she cried. "I know that's what Bradley thinks—how could you believe such a terrible thing about a woman you love?—but I didn't! I *didn't!*"

"You put the morphine in the chili," I persisted. "You knew Brad wouldn't touch it, because he was allergic to tomatoes. You just had to wait for Martin to come home and eat the chili and you'd be rid of your husband. You tried to murder him before he tried to murder you!"

"Oh, my," Victoria said. "That *would* explain why Martin is so angry."

"But I didn't do that," Suzanne sobbed.

I ignored the obvious lie. "In fact," I said, "I'm guessing Martin was already half-dead before he pulled the trigger on you. He didn't come home, shoot you, and then settle in for a little football and beer. He'd already eaten his poisoned dinner and was watching the game when he heard something upstairs. You killed him *first.*"

"We had fallen asleep," Bradley said, sounding weary. He had moved around from behind me so I could see his face. He looked as tired as he sounded—tired of holding onto secrets for so many years, maybe. "I woke up and heard the TV downstairs. I knew we had to get out of there before he found us, so I shook Suzanne. But she—" He shrugged. "I'd forgotten that it was a bad idea to wake her up suddenly. She had nightmares, and she always came out of a sound sleep screaming. That's what Martin heard. He was upstairs with the gun before we could get out of bed."

"And downstairs, already staggering, before he could leave the house," I said. "He had no intention of staying there with the two of you dead. But the morphine overtook him while he was in the kitchen, trying to get out the back door."

Bradley was staring at Suzanne. "How could you *do* that?" he whispered. "I would have taken you away from him. I would have kept you safe."

"How could you hate me so much?" she wailed. Weeping, she stumbled back into the house.

"Oh, dear," said Victoria. "Such a nasty thing to discover."

Bradley was looking after Suzanne with an expression of utter wretchedness on his face. "God. And I still love her," he muttered.

I said, "Maybe you—" but he cut me off.

"No," he said. "She killed a man." And he stalked around the side of the house to go pace back and forth across the front yard and frighten passersby.

"I'll go talk to her," Victoria said.

I looked at her curiously. I had discovered the truth, which was what Bradley had said Martin wanted. Did that mean Martin would be at peace? Did that mean all my ghosts would disappear? But Victoria looked the same as ever, brightly colored and almost fleshly. "You realize this might mean the end of Martin's hold on you," I said slowly. "You realize that, once he finds out what I've discovered, you might all dissipate."

I expected her to show a moment's sadness, but she nodded firmly. "Good. Time for us to move on. We'd all be glad of the rest. But as long as we're still here, I'm going to go comfort that girl."

I watched her go, wondering if I should join the conversation, but not ready to hear Suzanne's protestations of innocence one more time. Before I could go back inside, the neighbor from Janet's yard waved me over.

"Hello!" she called. "Come introduce yourself. I'm Marianne."

I wondered if she had just noticed me having an excited conversation with my collection of wraiths—whom she probably couldn't see—and if that had led her to deduce that I was crazy. But as I strolled up to the tangled thicket dividing our yards, I saw nothing but friendly interest on her face, which was tan and cheerful. She looked to be in her early thirties, with streaked blonde hair and a trim figure. She was wearing gardening clothes at the moment, but it was easy to imagine that she spent most of her days in tailored suits. She had that sort of professional air.

"I'm Erica," I said. "I don't think I've seen you before. I've scarcely met any of the neighbors."

She gave a little sigh. "None of us gets to know our neighbors in these busy times," she said. "And I've been traveling. But I heard the haunted house had found a tenant for the summer, and I'm glad to see you're still here. Any trouble with ghosts?"

So happily worded! So easy to answer in the affirmative without admitting my affinity for the dead. "No trouble," I replied. "I love the house."

She rested her rake in the dirt and folded her arms on the handle. "So do I," she said. "I inherited four properties from my aunt, and these two are my favorites." She gestured at my house and then her own.

Ah, so Marianne was the niece who still owned the house that had once been Suzanne's. I supposed Janet had been renting all this time. "You must have been pretty young when the murders occurred," I said.

"Sixteen," she replied. "But my Aunt Janet talked about them all the time. She just couldn't get over Suzanne's death."

"Aunt Janet," I repeated.

Marianne nodded. "She lived here right up until the day she died. Personally, I think I'd have moved away from a place where I was so tormented by tragedy, but that was Janet for you. A little obsessive."

Janet had *died*? Janet was *dead*? Wait a minute, wait a minute. "I'm confused," I said. "Who was Janet? And she used to own *both* these houses?"

Marianne shook her head. "No, she owned mine. Suzanne owned yours. They were sisters. Janet inherited yours when Suzanne died, and I got everything five years ago when Janet passed away."

I was staring at her. "Sisters…"

"I never knew Suzanne all that well, but Janet was strange. Jumpy. My mom said it was because her husband had beaten her up all the time and so any loud noise would scare her. He was killed in a car accident a year or two before Suzanne was murdered. Aunt Janet was never really sane after that. To be honest, it was something of a relief when she died."

I felt a moment's profound dizziness as my mind recalibrated everything I knew. Martin's chili had been poisoned by someone who had known Bradley wouldn't eat it because of his allergies—and that Suzanne wouldn't touch it because it contained meat. Surely a sister would know both those things. Janet had mentioned she was an ER nurse, so she could have had access to morphine even if there hadn't been leftover pills stashed in Martin's medicine cabinet. Janet still hated the husband who had abused her and didn't want to see Suzanne's life ruined in a similar way. *Janet* had killed Martin. Suzanne was innocent, just as she'd said.

"I'm sorry," I said to Marianne. "I've just remembered I need to make a phone call. So good to talk to you!" And I left her staring after me as I ran to the house.

I started shouting as soon as I was in the kitchen. Victoria looked up in astonishment from the cookbook I had left open on the counter.

"Erica, what in the world—"

"It was Janet!" I called, racing past her. "She poisoned the chili!" I tripped up the stairway, where Edison was lying in wait.

"Martin killed me," he complained. "Just as surely as if he'd pushed me."

"Sorry about that," I panted, and kept going. "Martin!" I called as I dashed toward the third bedroom. "Martin! I know what happened!"

Suzanne was there, flung face down on the bed, sobbing. Bradley stood over by the window, his hands balled into fists, his face filled with both fury and longing. "She didn't do it," I said breathlessly.

Bradley stared at me. "What?" Suzanne hiccupped and rolled over on her side to give me a drenched but hopeful glance.

I felt the air chill behind me, and I spun around to confront the half-formed darkness that was Martin. "You *were* murdered," I said, speaking very rapidly. "But not by Suzanne. Her sister Janet put the drugs in your soup."

Suzanne sat all the way up. "Janet?"

I nodded. "She loved you. She hated him."

Before anyone else could speak, Martin emitted a roar so terrifying that the house actually seemed to shake. It was suddenly zero in the room; for a moment I couldn't see. I shut my eyes and covered my ears and spent a moment shivering with unutterable cold.

Then the noise was gone. The room had warmed back to its usual cool temperature. I opened my eyes, and not a shadow remained.

Bradley was sitting beside Suzanne on the bed. His arms were wrapped around her shoulders and she was crying into his chest. "I'm so sorry," he murmured over and over. "So sorry. I love you so very much—"

I left them to their tearful confessions and went to look for the others. But Lizzie wasn't in my bedroom, and Edison wasn't on the stairs. Charlotte wasn't in the living room, and Victoria wasn't in the kitchen. I had the sudden conviction that, for the first time since I'd stepped inside this house, I was truly alone.

I ran up the stairs again, but Brad and Suzanne were no longer in the third bedroom. And the place actually felt as warm as a house ought to feel on a summer day.

I never saw any of the ghosts again, not even Janet. Now and then, just in case they were still nearby but out of my realm of vision, I would let PBS play all night long on the downstairs television. Occasionally I borrowed a children's book from the library and read it out loud, just in case Lizzie was listening. I still left cookbooks open in the kitchen. But none of them came back to visit; the house was peaceful.

I signed the papers that turned my husband into my ex-husband. Much more civilized than slipping him poison.

I told Marianne I'd be interested in buying the house if she was willing to sell, and she had a price to me the next day. Well within my means, now that Steve and I had divided our property.

But I was lonely. The house was too big for me to live in alone. I decided it was time to get a cat.

# Chief Executed Officers

It's one thing to wish a man dead. It's another to discover his bloody corpse in his expensive leather office chair when you go in to bring him his morning mail.

I had always hoped that, if ever confronted with the evidence of horrific violence, I would utter a faint gasp and sink to the ground in a graceful faint, but ladylike did not appear to be my normal operating mode. Upon seeing Dalton Bettis slumped behind his desk, his throat cut and his head askew, I shrieked like a soprano. A scream is more productive than a swoon any day. About a dozen of my coworkers instantly came running, and within five minutes we had fifteen people crowded into the doorway of Dalton's office, staring and speculating.

"We have to call the police."

"Who was the first one in the building this morning?"

"Is that the suit he had on yesterday? Do you think he's been here all night?"

And then, the whisper, the dread, the one question no one wanted to ask out loud.

"Do you think he was killed by whoever killed Jack Peterson?"

Within the hour, these were some of the same questions the police were asking. The twenty-seven—now twenty-six—employees of Ciexi Inc. were individually interviewed by a cadre of homicide detectives, while forensics types dusted and x-rayed and photographed for clues. Since I'd discovered the body, I was one of the first up. My interrogator was a heavy-set, humorless woman who had to be at least part Pobestani, judging by the yellowish cast of her skin and the fact that she had no visible body hair. We sat in the large, sterile conference room, which was not conducive to intimacy, and tried to communicate.

"Detective Falmer." I greeted her by name as I took my seat, since I remembered her from the last investigation. This was not much of a feat on my part. It had been only a week ago, and she was hard to forget.

I perhaps was not as memorable. She consulted her notes. "Lorelai Landis," she read, then looked up at me with intelligent gray eyes. "I understand you're the one who found Mr. Bettis this morning. Describe the scene for me."

I hadn't paused long to take in details; my memory had mostly retained the impression of lots of blood and a gash across Dalton's throat. No, I hadn't touched anything in the room. No, I hadn't noticed whether the state-of-the-art locks on the office doors had been tampered with before I arrived, and the winking red light on the surveillance camera had seemed to be in operation. I hadn't bothered to verify for myself.

"Were you the first one to see Mr. Bettis this morning?"

"I think so. No one else mentioned coming across a dead body, at any rate."

She frowned at my inappropriate levity. "Did you notice anything odd about his office when you went in—anything out of place, file drawers rifled, computer open to an unlikely site?"

"No."

"Were any windows open?"

I shook my head. "They're all sealed. Unbreakable, supposedly, but last year one of them cracked when Jack threw a chair at it."

Her sharp eyes sharpened. "That would be Jack Peterson, who was found murdered at his house last week."

"That's right."

"Was he in the habit of throwing chairs?"

"He was in the habit of expressing himself forcefully."

She glanced at her notes again. Someone else had interviewed me last time, asking the inevitable question: *Can you think of anyone who would have wanted to murder Jack Peterson?* My answer had been flippant. *I can't think of anyone who didn't.* Hadn't seemed smart at the time. Seemed less smart now as Detective Falmer no doubt read my comments from the file.

"How about Dalton Bettis?" she asked. "Was he in the habit of expressing himself forcefully?"

"Dalton Bettis kept a live boa constrictor in a glass case in his office," I said. "He kept twenty-six white mice in a cage. He used indelible ink to write his employees' names in the fur of the mice. When he was mad at someone, he fed the boa constrictor with the mouse who'd been named after that person. Would you call that forceful?"

Detective Falmer watched me in silence for a moment. "I take it you weren't particularly fond of him."

"I used to say there were really only five people I hated in the world," I said. Rash and stupid to admit, but I had a fabulous alibi, so I could say what I wanted. "Now two of them are dead."

"Who are the others?"

"Lola Arberry. Rance Cotton. Betty Baxter."

This time she didn't have to consult her notes. "The three executive vice presidents of Ciexi."

"Now that the CEO and the president are dead," I said, "they're the only ones left that all the employees are united in despising."

"Seems to me people might consider quitting a better option than murder," Detective Falmer said.

I shrugged. "Seems to me one office is much like another, and most CEOs are despicable," I said. "If you're going to feel like killing someone, maybe you should stick with the one you've already endured long enough to know you won't."

"That's cynical."

"That's me."

"So where were you last night between 8 p.m. and midnight?"

I gave her the widest, happiest smile she'd probably ever seen in her whole dour existence. "I was on live TV," I said.

I hadn't wanted to be on television. I had insisted to my best friend Renata that I didn't want to be part of her stupid community-access cable show which, this month, consisted of a call-in book discussion group. Unfortunately for me, I had not only read the book, I wasn't hospitalized with pneumonia, as was Renata's other reliable and semi-literate friend. So there I was on Channel 147, or whatever it was, blathering on about foreshadowing and subplot, while Dalton Bettis was bleeding all over his monogrammed shirt and tailor-made Italian suit.

Some days you just get lucky.

It was pretty much impossible to get any work done that day, what with the ongoing interrogations and the cluttering of the hallways by police and crime scene investigators.

Looked like another week where we would not meet our shipping deadlines, which would cause consternation and coronaries among our clients. Nonetheless, the mood in the office was generally upbeat, since the passing of Dalton Bettis improved everyone's life by a considerable margin. Even more than Jack Peterson's death, and that was saying something. Now and then—in snatched conversations in the lunchroom and whispered discussions in remote cubicles—someone would say, "What do you think will happen to all of us? Will the company have to shut down?" But no one really seemed too upset at the prospect. We might all be out job hunting by next week but, by God, Dalton Bettis was dead! It was one of those trade-offs that seemed eminently worthwhile.

The mood didn't really turn somber until Lola Arberry turned up dead the next morning. She'd been found in her car in the garage attached to her health club. Like Dalton, like Jack, she had had her throat cut. Detective Falmer brought this news as she returned to the office to continue the on-site investigation.

At this point, the pattern was impossible to miss. Somebody was working his—or her—way through the top leadership of Ciexi. Was there a grudge merely against the executive committee, or did someone hate the whole lot of us? Rance and Betty were right to suddenly feel a cold breath of terror on their necks, we all agreed, but who knew where the murderer would stop? Would *everyone* at Ciexi be eliminated? Detective Falmer shut the offices until further notice, despite Rance's protests that operations *must* continue or life on Earth would all but come to a halt. The rumor was that Betty had hired a bodyguard and Rance had demanded police protection.

But who would take care of the rest of us, if the rest of us were at risk?

I stepped out of the building and headed straight to Victor Denning's office.

Kibbi was sitting in the outer office when I arrived, and his face showed a complicated expression when he saw me. Part pleasure, part surprise, part wariness. He'd been sitting right there the last time I'd come visiting, so he'd heard virtually my entire fight with Victor. Like Victor, Kibbi was full-blooded Pobestani, with the same sleek bald head, deep amber skin, and spooky gray eyes. But he was short, smiling, shy, and just this side of goofy. Nothing like Victor. Don't let anyone tell you all Pobestani are alike. There are race commonalities, sure, but the dissimilarities can be spectacular.

"Lorelai," Kibbi said. Pleasure must have won out over surprise, because he jumped up and came around the desk to hug me. I hugged him back, inhaling that faint herbal sage scent that all Pobestani seemed to have in common. On Victor it was almost irresistible. On Kibbi, merely comforting. "We've missed you!"

"Don't get too attached, I'm not back for good," I said crisply, pulling back and letting go. "I assume he's in his office? Can I go in?"

Kibbi tried to assume the professional aspect of a human secretary. Didn't work with his wide grin and his soft face. "Is he expecting you?"

"Isn't he always?" I retorted, and entered Victor's office without knocking.

He was standing there waiting for me.

At least, that was the impression he gave. It was always the impression he gave, any time someone entered his immediate field of vision. There was that moment of stillness as he absorbed the fact that you had appeared—yes, *you*, the one he had heard so much about, the one he had been thinking of lately—and then the smile, the look of explosive happiness. The odd gray eyes darkened to warmth, the angular amber face slanted into happiness. I had met maybe a hundred Pobestani, and not one of them was as beautiful as Victor Denning.

"Lorelai," he said. "My heart returns."

I shut the door, hoping to keep Kibbi out of the conversation. He had exceptionally good hearing, though, so a few inches of cheap wood probably wouldn't do the trick.

"I haven't returned," I said. "I'm still not speaking to you."

"Then why are you here, if not to speak?" He tilted his head back to assess me. "You don't appear to be dressed for seduction, but if that's—"

"No," I said sharply. "I need your services. Your *professional* services," I clarified.

Pobestani don't have eyebrows, so Victor couldn't lift his, but the skin on his forehead wrinkled as he widened his eyes. "You need a private detective," he said.

"Perhaps you've heard," I said. "We've had three murders at Ciexi."

"I'd heard about two," he replied. "Who's the third?"

"Lola Arberry. This morning."

Victor didn't look horrified or frightened or outraged. Somewhat reprehensibly, he appeared amused. Pobestani have strange ideas about death and rebirth and the eternal place of the soul in the universe, and other beliefs about the afterlife that I don't quite get. They're one of those death-is-a-doorway people. It makes them relatively peaceful when it comes to dying, but I'd think it would make it hard to ever come to closure.

Come to think of it, closure on any issue wasn't Victor's strong suit.

"Jack Peterson, Dalton Bettis and Lola Arberry *all* dead?" Victor said softly. "And how are you celebrating?"

"Well, that's the thing," I said. "Everyone at the office is wondering if this is where the murders stop, or if all the rest of us are about to be slaughtered, too. Makes me a little less thrilled about the glorious present and a little more worried about the uncertain future."

The smile snapped from his face like it was broken off. "You're in danger?" he asked, short and sharp.

"I don't know," I said. "Until we know who the killer is, we won't know who else has been targeted. The police have been called in, but—" I shrugged. I didn't have to elaborate. Victor had an exquisite sense of contempt for the metropolitan police force. Or at least for the humans on the force, and they were in the vast majority. It had never ceased to amaze me that Pobestani, with their superior gifts for uncovering the truth, solving riddles, and ruthlessly taking logical action, hadn't become the elite crime-fighting units in all major cities. But in fact, you rarely found a pureblood Pobestani on the police force. Basic human mistrust and jealousy, I suppose. An unwillingness to admit that the aliens could be better at something than we were.

"Who do *you* think the killer is?" Victor asked.

I shrugged again. "It could be almost anyone! That is, anyone who knew all three of them—most likely one of their employees or one of their clients. That leaves twenty-five suspects near at hand and, I don't know, fifty or sixty with less access but just as much motive."

"The police must have eliminated some of the suspects already merely by checking alibis. For instance, you could not have committed the murder of Dalton Bettis, so I would think you would be off the list for the others."

I stared. "Why would you think I couldn't kill Dalton? I hated him enough."

"You were broadcasting a cable television show while he was being killed."

"How did you know that?" I demanded.

He smiled. "I have an acquaintance at the police department who supplied me with some details of the murder, such as estimated time of death."

That was a given. Victor knew everything about everything that happened in the city, and he had friends everywhere. "Not about time of death. About me and the television show."

"Lorelai. I watched it, of course. I always know where you are and what you're doing."

"You better not be stalking me, you arrogant *poblenko* prick," I said fiercely, angry enough to use inexcusable language. "I *will* call the cops on you, and I have friends on the police force, too."

"I would not do such a thing. You have told me to stay away, and so I stay away. It is just that I cannot fail to hear you still. Feel you still." He touched the side of his smooth skull, then the area of his chest where his heart should reside. If he had a heart. Oh, Pobestani *do* have hearts, just like ours—they're our genetic cousins, after all—but there were days I didn't think Victor's did more than pump that rich foreign blood through his body. "I will always have a connection to you. I'm Pobestani and you're the love of my life."

It sounded like a line, but I knew it to be true. All Pobestani come prepackaged with certain features—ferocious intelligence, acute senses, honey-gold skin, and a whole smorgasbord of personality traits like loyalty, honesty, and dependability. They pair-bond for life, some of them finding their perfect complements when they're children, others not until they're mature and seasoned. I had been twenty-two, Victor ten years older, when we met five years ago. These days it hurt too much to remember how he looked at me that first time he saw me—stricken, ravished, euphoric, all at once. It was painful to recall how the floor seemed to disintegrate beneath my feet, like sand dissolving when a wave sweeps along the beach.

"*Anolishka*," he had whispered, as if he had thought he would never have cause to speak the syllables aloud. I knew enough about his race to recognize the word. *Soulmate.* All Pobestani hope to find theirs someday, and they know there will be only one in their lifetimes.

One soulmate. But many potential bedmates. You think *loyalty* and *fidelity* mean the same thing until you find your Pobestani lover in bed with someone else.

"Funny, that naked blonde was sure looking like the love of your life when I caught you with her last month," I said.

Victor smiled again, in no way discomposed. "I tried to explain at the time. We have different customs, you and I. Once I understand where I transgress—at least, by your conventions—I can understand where to tread lightly in the future."

See there? Does that sound like a man who's telling you, *Darling, I'll never sleep with any girl but you as long as I live?* Not even remotely. Never, *never* have I met a man who can make me as mad as fast as Victor Denning can.

"Well, you can stomp around just as loud as you like because I'm not going to be dealing with any of your transgressions ever again," I said in a snotty voice. "And I didn't come here today to talk about you and me."

"Of course not," he said in a soothing voice that made it clear he was thinking I had jumped at the first legitimate excuse I had found to admit him back into my life. "You came to talk about murder."

"I thought maybe you could find out who did the killings," I said. "From what I can tell, the police don't have any real leads. You could figure this thing out in three days flat."

He watched me gravely. "Are you sure you want this crime solved?" he asked.

"Why wouldn't I? Especially if somebody's working his way through the whole staff roster! I don't want to be next."

He shook his head. "That's possible, of course, but it seems unrealistically ambitious. It's more likely that a disgruntled employee—or customer, as you say—has targeted the members of the executive committee."

"Who all deserved to suffer great torture and despair," I said with a sigh, "but probably didn't deserve to die. I think killing them is worse than *being* them, if you understand what I mean. So, yeah, I want the crime solved."

"If the murderer is a coworker," he said, his voice even softer, "it may very well be a friend. Someone you care about deeply. Do you want to see that person suffer for these actions?"

I stared at him. Was it possible he was warning me off? Was it possible he already knew who the culprit was? Was it possible ...

"Victor," I said in a strangled voice, "please tell me you haven't been killing off Ciexi's whole C-suite just because you thought it would make me happy."

He laughed, and I felt myself relax. If he'd committed the murders, he would have admitted it right now. Even police don't make Pobestani take lie-detector tests. They just inquire whether or not an individual has taken a specific action. They get the true confession every time. The trick with a Pobestani is to ask the right question.

"Lorelai, I love you," he said. "But I am not yet so desperate that I would kill a person to win you back. Or two or three."

"Then you'll help me?" I said. "You'll investigate the case?"

"Ah, well, I *am* desperate enough to charge you a steep price for that," he said.

I eyed him uncertainly. He was still smiling. This made me more uncertain. "What price?"

He came near enough to take my hand. I hated myself for wanting to melt into his arms. This close, I could smell that sun-warmed sage odor, his body's natural cologne. I had to discipline a desire to kiss him madly.

"Come back to me," he said.

I jerked myself free. "No."

He recaptured my hand, holding on more tightly this time. "Just for a week," he said. "Just long enough for me to prove how much I love you. After that we can discuss long-term possibilities and mutual conditions."

I wrenched my hand away, feeling like a layer of skin came with it. I couldn't tell if I was angrier at him for the suggestion or myself for wanting to agree. "*No,*" I said even more hotly. "I'm sorry I asked. I'm sure the police will be able to handle everything."

His expression now was entirely sober. "As you say, the chances are good I can solve this crime in three days or less," he said. "Who knows how long it will take the police? Who knows who else might be killed while they botch and dither? If you hire me, you could very well be saving a life—or two. Do you really want to have someone's death on your conscience?"

Add another item to my long list of reasons it's a bad idea to take a Pobestani lover. Their skills of emotional manipulation are second to none. Or maybe that's just Victor's own particular talent.

"I wouldn't even think of sleeping with someone who offered me a bargain like that," I said in a lofty voice and stalked toward the door. "Goodbye, Victor. I'm sorry I came by."

I exited, slammed the door behind me, and stormed past Kibbi toward the outer door. The look on Kibbi's face was a mix of astonishment and rue.

Just as I'd expected, he'd heard every word.

Renata and I met for drinks at a trendy club with low lighting, lots of mirrors, and some odd-smelling pinkish smoke that mostly hovered near the floor, puddling around our ankles. Pobestani bar. The aliens go in for lights and colors and what I think of as "undulation." All the visual input gives me a headache fast, but the Pobestani can't get enough of it.

Renata had picked the venue. She's one-quarter Pobestani and three-quarters polyglot human, a racial heritage that has gifted her with beautifully shaped facial bones, skin the color of cocoa butter, and soulful dark eyes. Bad hair, though. Thin and frizzy and the color of oak, flyaway and untamable. The hair contributes to her general air of ditziness, which most people find charming and few people realize masks a mind that's as sharp as jagged glass.

We were drinking some alcoholic beverage that tasted like smoky gingerbread and had an extremely high proof.

Never knew what you'd get at a Pobestani bar. But it was awfully good.

"Here's the ethical question of the day," I said. "Should you have sex with someone to prevent someone else from getting killed?"

Renata sipped from her drink and looked as thoughtful as she could with stray fronds of hair drifting across her high forehead. "Depends," she said. "Is the person you're potentially having the sex with also going to be doing the killing?"

"I don't think so. Not utterly positive."

"Because, naturally, you wouldn't want to contemplate intimacy with someone who was capable of premeditated murder," she added.

"Naturally."

"Is the person who might be killed someone you care about? Someone you would be sorry to see dead?"

"Nooooo," I said thoughtfully. "Still, to fail to take action to prevent someone else's murder seems unconscionable, don't you think?"

"We're still determining that," Renata said. "Do you have strong feelings of revulsion for the potential romantic partner?"

I sighed. "Not at all."

"So you believe that if you sleep with an attractive individual whom you don't actually despise, the life of someone you don't care about might be spared. While I'm still unclear on how that exact cause-and-effect could actually translate from theory into fact, I can't see anything wrong with the basic suggestion."

I sighed again. "Victor says if I come back to him, he'll figure out who's killing off the top executives at Ciexi before anyone else dies."

Renata nodded again. She had never found her own *anolishka,* though she had managed to have a pretty interesting time of it while she conducted the search. She had enough Pobestani blood in her to hope she someday found her perfect match and was human enough to doubt she ever would. "He came to you and said this?"

"I went to him and asked for help."

Unlike Victor, Renata had eyebrows—thin, delicate arches over her big eyes—and she raised them now. "Well, I'm not surprised he thought you might agree. It would give you a way to return to the relationship without losing your self-respect. Doing something for the public good, and not because you *wanted* to sleep with him again."

"I turned him down."

"Of course you did! He was clumsy and obvious."

I toyed with the stem of my glass. "But now I'm thinking—won't I feel terrible if Rance or Betty dies and I know I could have saved them? Or what if someone else at the office is killed? Someone I like?"

"Don't worry about it," Renata advised. "Victor will solve the case. I'm sure he's working on it right now."

"He *is?* After I said no?"

Renata looked surprised. "You asked him to do it. He loves you. He expressed conditions that represented his preference, but they were just intended to make his feelings known. As soon as you asked for his help, there was no question that he would give it. No matter what you did next."

For the first time in a month, my heart actually softened toward Victor. I wasn't ready to forgive him for the blonde betrayal just yet, but I could entertain the thought that he might not deserve my undying hatred. "Then maybe this case will be solved by the time the office reopens."

Renata toasted me with her gingerbread drink. "And you can feel virtuous about saving a few lives."

"That still leaves the problem of what to do about Victor. For the long term."

Renata smiled. It was the smile, from her whole repertoire, that I always thought of as pure Pobestani—knowing, wicked, and bone-deep amused. "For the short term," she corrected. "Long term we already know."

"We do?"

"You and Victor forever."

I rolled my eyes. "I don't believe that *anolishka* crap," I said, although I secretly did, or wished I did, anyway. "One love for the whole of your life."

"Not just this life," she corrected. "The next life. The life after that. And many lifetimes before this one, too. Haven't you always wondered why you recognized Victor the moment you saw him? You walked the wheel with him in another time."

I signaled the waiter to bring me another of those intoxicating drinks. Clearly I'd be taking a taxi home. "Well, I'm off the wheel for good," I said. "Victor can just find somebody else to walk with."

Renata was laughing. "He won't," she assured me, "and neither will you."

To test Renata's theory—and for no other reason—I returned to Victor's the next afternoon. Kibbi gave me a big smile and waved me into Victor's inner office.

The whole corkboard wall behind his desk was covered with timetables, pictures of dead people, employee ID photos and blueprints. A cursory glance revealed that what was on display were the relevant players and places connected to the Ciexi murders. Victor was standing utterly still before the wall, one arm crossed over his chest, one hand lifted to tap his chin. When I stepped inside, he turned to give me that where-have-you-been-my-whole-life smile. To cover the fact that it made my insides all fluttery, I scowled.

"I thought you weren't going to start investigating this case until I started putting out," I said rudely.

"I shall take the conclusion as a given at some point in the future, no matter how distant, and begin upholding my part of the bargain now," he said.

I came deeper into the room and scanned the pictures and the drawings, not much discomposed by seeing Dalton's and Jack's corpses. It was still a satisfaction to realize they were dead. "Where'd you get the crime scene stuff?"

"I told you I had friends among the police."

"Have you discovered anything?"

"In fact, I have." He turned his attention back to the corkboard and waved a hand. "The three murders were committed at three different sites, each offering a different kind of rather sophisticated security. Yet the murderer managed to outwit the locks and sensors at all three locations. This argues a high level of intelligence and possibly a mathematical or scientific bent."

"Okay," I said, though it argued nothing of the sort to me.

"In each case, the victim's throat was cut from behind, indicating some upper body strength. But the fact that the killer could get close enough to perform the deed also indicates that the murderer did not seem threatening to the victims."

"So—someone who looked weak—or someone who was short—or a woman," I said.

Victor gave me one quick look, brimming with amusement. "I think Dalton Bettis and Jack Peterson always found women threatening," he said.

"Yes, but not *physically* threatening," I said, grinning back.

Victor studied the wall again. "Meanwhile, the police have found nothing at any of the murder sites. Not only no murder weapon and no prints, but *nothing*. No DNA evidence. No nail clippings. No stray hairs." He pivoted slowly and turned to look at me. "No hairs," he repeated.

I felt my mouth drop open. "But—you think—"

He counted on his fingers. "Deeply intelligent. Generally considered nonthreatening. Devoid of body hair. I think your killer is a Pobestani."

"But—but—Pobestani don't murder people! I mean, *ever!* They've been living with humans for decades now and I can't think of a single time when a Pobestani instigated violence against a person! Sure, there have been cases where Pobestani killed humans, but the humans were always the ones who started the fight. Always."

"I know of three exceptions in the past fifteen years in this city alone, but, in general, you're correct," Victor said. "So for a Pobestani to have carried out these murders, he would have had to believe he—or someone he loved—had been harmed by the victims. And that he was enacting justice."

I rubbed my eyes. I was remembering that Victor had warned me that I might find something I didn't like if he investigated this case. "There are a handful of Pobestani who work at Ciexi," I said in a tired voice.

"Five," Victor said. "I've already invited each of them to come in and answer some questions."

I dropped my hand and stared at him. "And they've agreed?"

He nodded. "Of course."

"And the police have agreed? You've checked with Detective Falmer?"

He smiled. "We need not bother her until we've discovered something of interest."

"But why would these guys be willing to come in and talk to a private detective if you don't have the law behind you..." My words trailed off.

Because they were Pobestani. Because they didn't think like humans, in terms of laws and lawyers and courts and subpoenas. Because they were governed by an entirely different social compact of collaboration and respect.

"What will you do if one of them confesses?" I asked in a hollow voice.

"I imagine it will be clear to everyone what to do next," he said.

I couldn't guess what he meant, but I nodded, as if I understood. "When do the interviews start?"

He checked his watch. "Joey Larser arrives in fifteen minutes. Would you like to stay?"

The first three interviews took place in the next hour, one right after the other. Everyone was eerily friendly, even jovial, as Kibbi escorted them in. Joey and the second suspect, a Pobestani woman named Evelyn, had met Victor before and greeted him with big smiles and warm handshakes. The third suspect, a slim boy who worked in our mailroom, was a stranger even to me. He'd only been at Ciexi for about a month. Still, he came into the office wreathed in smiles, clasped Victor's hand as if he was a long-lost mentor, and smiled at me so broadly his toasted-gold skin furrowed into wrinkles all around his smooth face.

Victor had only a few questions for each. "Did you kill Dalton Bettis? Did you kill Jack Peterson? Did you kill Lola Arberry?" He asked about each one separately, he explained to me later, because if he merely said, *Did you kill these three?* and our suspect had only committed one murder, he could honestly reply in the negative.

They all replied in the negative anyway.

More questions. "Do you know who did commit these murders? Do you have any knowledge about these crimes at all?"

In each case, that last question elicited almost identical responses, offered in the most helpful voices imaginable. "Well, now, I know what days the murders occurred. And I know what the police have told us."

So Victor amended his inquiry. "Did you have any involvement with any of these crimes, even the slightest?"

No. And no. And no.

These three, at least, appeared to be innocent of murder. We all shook hands again as they left, one by one. I sat in Victor's office and realized the sun was almost down.

"Who's next?" I asked.

"Lanny Shaw, but not 'til tomorrow morning," he said. "Also Gwen somebody, right after Lanny."

"So—you think one of those two is the killer?"

He looked at me. His gray eyes looked compassionate, and I realized he felt sorry for me. The interrogations, simple and brief as they'd been, had left me feeling drained and a little sick to my stomach. It wasn't the mere act of asking questions and listening to the answers that was so exhausting, of course—it was the emotional stress of waiting for someone to declare himself a killer. It was the balled-up uncertainty that had made a dense shape in my abdomen. It was the sense that I had to be ready to jump up and tackle a self-confessed murderer as he made a break for freedom.

Victor didn't look particularly tired or upset. In fact, he had assumed a greater air of calm than he usually wore, and even his ordinary state was preternatural. "Possibly Lanny or Gwen is the killer," he said. "Possibly not. As you have said before, it could be a client. It could be a former employee. This is just our best short list."

I heaved myself to my feet. I had been slumped in one of Victor's comfortable office chairs and I felt as if I had gained a ton and a half during the course of one guilt-ridden, anxious day. "Then I'll be back tomorrow morning to hear what the others have to say," I replied.

Victor moved smoothly to cut me off at the door. "Let me take you out to dinner to reward you for your exertions," he said.

"I don't think so," I said huffily.

He laughed. "I promise. No additional importuning. Merely food, possibly some alcohol, and a chaste goodbye at your door."

Sounded good, but I was a skeptic. What sounded good in theory so often was wrenchingly bad in execution. "How about a chaste goodbye right here?" I said.

"How about it?" he murmured. Before I realized what he intended, he swept me into his arms, laying his cheek against mine and holding me tightly to his chest. I was almost overwhelmed with conflicting feelings of sadness, desire, comfort, and the sense of coming home. Was Renata right? Had he held me like this, just so, in other times, in other lives? Was Victor's embrace the one place I truly belonged?

I wasn't ready for it to be true. I stamped on his foot, yanked myself out of his arms, and flung open the door in one grand swoop of movement. Victor made no move to stop me, merely watched me with a lurking smile. "Goodbye, quite chastely," he called, but I barely heard the words in the crash of the door into the frame. Kibbi stared as I practically ran past. I was crying by the time I climbed into a cab.

During the short ride back to my house I kept rubbing my face where Victor's beardless cheek had lain against mine. The hug had been so brief—surely it was my imagination now that my skin had picked up his scent of tumbled sage.

In the morning I was back, dressed in dark colors and spiny jewelry that would puncture someone's skin if he pressed too close. I'd also worn ankle boots with high spiked heels, the better to kick or trample someone. These accouterments were not lost on Victor, who merely grinned when I stepped through his door.

"Just in time," he said. "Lanny will be here in five minutes."

But Lanny, asked point-blank if he had committed the Ciexi murders, told us he had not. Gwen gave the same answer. I was both relieved and discouraged to find no murderer among the people I knew. Who had done the killings, then? On the bright side, no one else had died in the last two days. Maybe we were done with slaughter.

"What do we do next?" I asked Victor rather glumly once Kibbi had escorted Gwen out. "I can get you a pretty comprehensive list of companies we've done business with in the last two years."

"First, we eat something," Victor said, summoning Kibbi back into his office. "Can you get some sandwiches and some bottled water for Lorelai and me?" he said. "And some for yourself, too. We'll all sit here and brainstorm a while."

"I'm not hungry," I said automatically. I was, actually, but I was making a point: I was not willing to submit to *any* kind of caregiving from Victor.

"Sandwiches for three," Victor said. "Kibbi and I will eat them if you find yourself without an appetite."

There was a little deli on the ground floor below Victor's third-story office. Kibbi would be back in ten minutes. I sighed—lately I had been doing that more often than was attractive—and stretched my high-heeled feet before me. "The problem with the client list is that Jack, Dalton, and Lola usually dealt with different customers," I said. "So while a client might certainly have a wish to kill one of them, he probably wouldn't have known all three of them well enough to want them dead."

"Maybe it's not a client, then," Victor said. "Back to the employee theory. Maybe we're looking at the wrong people."

"Maybe we're asking the wrong questions," I said.

"Those are the only questions," Victor said firmly. "'Did you kill these people? Do you know who did?' Those should elicit the right answers."

"Should, should, should," I said impatiently. "What if we've come up against the only Pobestani in the universe who can lie? We could ask the right questions all day and still get the wrong answers."

"I realize we must consider all the possibilities," Victor said gravely, "but considering that one is a waste of time."

Arrogant, manipulative, *and* condescending. I was very glad Victor was displaying all his least likable traits. It was making it easier for me to resist him. I decided not to answer this latest comment and sat there for a few minutes, brooding in silence. Victor flipped through files open on his desk.

"Something we haven't considered," he said, as if there had been no break in the conversation, "is former employees. Particularly those who have been fired or who left under less than ideal circumstances."

I straightened in my chair and shook my head. I could hear the outer door open as Kibbi returned. I said, "I can't think of a Pobestani employee who's left within the past eighteen months. Whether or not under protest."

"A human employee with a Pobestani lover," he suggested.

I tilted my head and gave him a hard look. "Just like you and me," I said. Kibbi was stepping through the door into the inner office, but I didn't care. His ears were so acute he would have heard this whole conversation even if he'd been sitting at his desk. "A Pobestani realizes his human lover is unhappy in her place of employment. Because loyalty is one of his defining characteristics, he thinks to make her happy by killing off her mean bosses, one by one."

"That could be the scenario," Victor said cautiously.

I leaned forward, staring into his wide gray eyes. Sometimes they seemed so expressive to me; sometimes, like now, they seemed shadowy and full of secrets. "Maybe I didn't phrase it exactly right the first day I came here," I said slowly. "Did you kill any of the three top executives at Ciexi?"

"I did not," Victor said.

"I did," Kibbi said, and handed me a sandwich.

The food fell from my nerveless hands as I stared up at Kibbi. His round, happy face looked worried but hopeful, the face of a puppy who's chewed up his owner's shoes but thinks perhaps his owner will understand there was an exceptionally good reason. "Kibbi," I whispered. "But why?"

"*Anolishka,*" he said, and gave me his usual loving smile.

I caught my breath. "Me? *Anolishka?*" I choked out. "Kibbi, I—"

But Victor spoke from across the room. "Not you," he said. "Me."

Kibbi was glancing between us, and again I was put in mind of canine metaphors, for he wore a look of doglike devotion. "I would do anything to make Victor happy," he said earnestly. "But only you make him happy. And I thought, how can I convince Lorelai to come back to us again?" He spread his arms. He was smiling. "And here you are."

"But Kibbi, I—I wouldn't have—I mean, to kill people just to drive me back into Victor's arms, that's—you can't—" Really, I had no idea how to explain why this was such a terrible idea. Anyone who had conceived of it would be hard to convince.

"I know it was wrong," he said, still earnestly. "I know what I have to do next."

He turned and hurried out the door. I jumped to my feet, intending to run after him, but quite suddenly, Victor was beside me, holding me close despite my unfriendly jewelry.

"Don't look," he said, and bent my head so that my eyes were against his chest. I struggled, but only until I heard the harsh report of a firearm going off in the outer office. I sagged against Victor as I realized that Kibbi must have shot himself. Had planned to shoot himself as soon as he was discovered, which he had assumed would be sooner rather than later. Had planned this whole series of events, this grand tragedy, from the first break-in at Jack Peterson's to the suicide this afternoon.

All for me.
All for Victor.
*Anolishka.*

I stayed 'til the police arrived, gave my statement, comported myself with far greater calm than I was really feeling. I refused to make eye contact with Victor, stayed as far away from him as I could while Detective Falmer and her troops scoured the offices and asked the same questions about four hundred times. The minute I was cleared to go, I was out the door, not even saying farewell to Victor. He made no attempt to stop me.

He always could tell when it was best to leave me alone.

I headed straight for Renata's and poured out the story, bursting into tears before I'd even dropped to the couch. She hugged me, fetched me a glass of wine, and listened to me tell the entire story over again from the beginning.

"I don't understand," I said, hiccupping as I finished my second glass of wine. "I thought—*anolishka*—I thought everybody found his own soulmate and lived happily ever after."

"Most Pobestani do find their *anolishka,*" Renata said gravely. "But sometimes it's one-sided—not often, but sometimes. It can lead to great heartache, but most often it becomes what you saw between Kibbi and Victor—deep friendship. The *anolishka* who does not love in return usually tries to display great kindness to the one who loves him. After all, he would hope for such treatment from his own *anolishka* if that person did not love him. Kibbi was content, you know. He spent part of every day with his soulmate. And he died trying to make Victor happy. He considered that a triumph."

"Yes, but—to murder people! For whatever reason! I can't—I mean—that's so extreme. So extremely *wrong.*"

"Which Kibbi knew. Which is why he killed himself at the end." That made me start crying again, so Renata gave me another big hug. "Don't be so sad," she said. "Kibbi knows that he goes to the Great Circle, where he waits to be called out again when the wheel spins his way. He believes that he will encounter Victor again in his next life, and the life after that. Death brings hope, not despair."

"Four people have died because of me," I sobbed, burying my face in one of her decorative pillows. I could feel the scratchy embroidery turn soggy with my tears. "And I wasn't even sorry the first three were *dead!* And now it's my *fault!* Don't talk to me about wheels and circles and soulmates! Everything is terrible! Everything will always be terrible from now until forever!"

Renata patted me on the shoulder. "Nothing is ever terrible for quite that long," she said.

Despite my guilt and grief, I managed to make it to work when the office re-opened two days later. As expected, literally no work was accomplished during the entire day, and neither Rance nor Betty seemed to expect it to be. They'd clearly spent the enforced holiday redrawing organizational charts and re-apportioning responsibility, for they bustled about the office having private conferences with key employees, informing them of their new roles and duties. They were officious and annoying but, on the whole, less evil than Dalton Bettis, and I found myself being glad that Kibbi had stopped his spree before working his way any farther through the executive committee. I mean, this whole thing was a tragedy wrapped around a nightmare, but that didn't entirely obscure the fact that Dalton Bettis was actually dead. While he sat in the Great Circle, awaiting his next call to life, the rest of us could go about actually enjoying ours.

It was a full week before I could bring myself to go see Victor.

He already had a new secretary in place, a woman who looked to be half Pobestani and a hundred-and-five years old. Her white hair was so thin I thought she'd be better to shave it all off completely, since the shape of her skull, distinctly visible, was regal and pleasing. Her eyes were sharp and her smile, though conditional, seemed ready to be welcoming if I proved worthy. I wondered if she had been the one to clean away all the blood. The outer office was spotless.

"Lorelai Landis," I introduced myself. "I was wondering if Victor Denning would be able to see me now."

"I'm sure he would," she said, and I walked right in.

He was standing in the middle of his office, facing the door, waiting for me. As he was always waiting for me. His smile was broader than the secretary's, but equally provisional. It was clear he was not entirely sure what to expect from me, but was braced for whatever might come.

"Lorelai," he said. *"Anolishka."*

"Did you know?" I asked him, coming to a complete halt just inside the room. I wondered if the new secretary had ears that were as good as Kibbi's and decided I didn't care. At any rate, it seemed likely she'd found her own soulmate some years in the past and was less likely to be intensely interested in everything that happened in Victor's personal life.

"Did I know what?" he replied.

"That Kibbi. That he felt that way about you."

"Yes."

"Did you realize he was the one who had committed the murders?"

He shook his head. "Not at first. I had begun to put the pieces together that morning, when our last two employee suspects didn't pan out. But even then it was only an inkling."

"Would you have taken the case if you *had* known?"

He looked surprised. "Of course."

"Knowing that Kibbi—your friend, your—whatever he was, this person who loved you—would be arrested and go to jail and maybe be put to death for what he'd done? You would have taken the case knowing that you would have done that to him?"

"Of course," he repeated. "Kibbi would have expected me to. He *did* expect me to, that's why he committed the crimes in the first place."

"And then—you didn't seem surprised—did you know he would feel obliged to kill himself? There at the end?"

Victor nodded. "It is common among our people who realize they have reached a grave impasse. It is clear this life has reached its useful stopping point. Time to end this one and move on to the next."

*Impasse* didn't seem like quite the right word to describe Kibbi's actions, but I couldn't think of a better one. I felt sad and small and hopelessly confused. "I'll never understand the Pobestani," I said. "You or any of them."

Victor smiled and took a step toward me. A small step, but it was definite forward motion. "I will be happy to explain," he said. "We can move from the general to the particular in a very short span of time."

"Maybe I don't want to know you any better," I said haughtily.

Another step closer, then one long stride. He was right beside me, lifting one hand to stroke my cheek. "And maybe you do," he said.

I closed my eyes briefly and realized I had swayed in his direction. I opened my eyes and stepped back, hostility flaring. "Don't try any of your Pobestani tricks," I warned.

He was laughing. "What tricks would those be?"

I clutched my purse tighter. "Well, I'm not sure exactly. The ones you're going to tell me about."

He put a hand on my shoulder and urged me to the door. "Tonight. Right now. Over dinner," he agreed. "I won't keep anything a secret."

The new secretary looked up when we came out and gave us a benevolent smile. She had decided she liked me after all. "Are you leaving for the day, then?" she asked, sounding as if she approved of such lax behavior.

"Oh, I think so," Victor said. "Lorelai and I have a great deal of catching up to do."

As soon as we stepped outside the door, Victor took my hand again, and I allowed him to keep it. I still wasn't sure if I believed in that Big Wheel, or whatever the Pobestani called it, and I was far from certain I would want to tread it over and over at Victor's side even if they were right about the endless cycle of death and rebirth. But in this lifetime? On this day? There was only person I wanted to walk with. One arm I wanted to feel around my shoulders. One kiss on my lips.

No choice but to go forward with his hand in mine.

# THE UNRHYMED COUPLETS OF
# THE UNIVERSE

Henry sipped from his morning coffee, gazing over the rim of the cup at the green plastic ball in the middle of the kitchen table. It had not been there twenty seconds previously. He had looked up from buttering his second piece of toast to find it sitting jauntily on top of the real estate section of the newspaper.

Henry was eighty-two years old, retired since he was seventy, a widower since he was seventy-six, and nothing much alarmed him or terrified him anymore. Certainly not a child's scuffed green ball, no matter how sudden its appearance. It didn't do anything interesting for the five minutes he watched it, so he eventually shrugged, stood up, and cleared the table. By the time he had finished rinsing out the coffee pot and loading the dishwasher, the ball was gone.

That evening while he watched television, a fat red pillow manifested itself beside him on the couch. It was edged with gold braid and looked like it belonged in a living room that was much fancier than anything Henry would find comfortable. Like the ball, it didn't stick around long. Before the next commercial break, it had vanished.

More random objects appeared at a somewhat faster rate the following day. The first one showed up while Henry was sitting at his desk, checking emails. He loved email. Never had to speak to a soul if you didn't feel like it, but you still had the sense of being connected to every person you'd ever met in your entire life, even the ones you didn't like so much. He was just typing a reply to his sister in Florida when he glanced over to find a small glass of water sitting at his right elbow. In the water was a thin paintbrush, and the residue of black paint had oozed from the bristles into the liquid, turning it a foggy gray. Henry couldn't think that these were the tools of a true artist; more likely they belonged to an old woman daubing at a heavy piece of pressed paper or a child experimenting with color.

They were gone before he'd thought about it too much, but he hadn't even stood up from the desk before the next apparition of the day arrived. It was a photo frame, holding a picture of a laughing family of five as they posed before a waterfall in what looked like a national park. Henry might not even have noticed it except that it blocked the photo of Ellen that he glanced at on a fairly regular basis. He pushed it aside carefully, in case his touch might contaminate it in some way and make it impossible for the frame to return to its rightful place—the way he'd always been taught the scent of a human would contaminate a baby bird or a wild rabbit and make its natural parents shun it forever. But he wanted to gaze at Ellen a moment before he quit the room for the day.

The photo on his desk was his favorite picture of her, out of what must be several hundred he had in photo albums and boxes. It showed her at a time when she was about fifty, and she'd just started coloring her hair to keep away the gray. Her face retained the laugh lines and character lines that had defined her so strongly, but the dye job returned the youthful look that the aging process had started to compromise. She was laughing, as she was laughing in most pictures. She looked ready to jump straight out of the frame, grab his arm, and tug him down the hall, out the door and off into some expedition. No one had ever had more energy than Ellen.

Some days he still missed her so much that it took him a moment to catch up on his breathing.

The photo of the strangers seemed to amuse her; at any rate, her face remained radiant as long as that second frame stayed on his desk. She was still smiling when it disappeared.

A box of Cracker Jacks showed up in the dining room while he was eating lunch. During the afternoon, Henry almost tripped over a single black shoe lying in the hallway that led to the back bathroom. The bathroom itself harbored a slim white candle—lit—set in a small crystal holder. That evening, while he watched the news, a current *Time* magazine appeared on the coffee table. Henry couldn't resist picking it up and flipping through it, reading the technology report and the movie reviews. While he held it in his hands, it vanished, leaving a faint tingle on his fingertips. He had been in the middle of an article about the upcoming election, and he was sorry not to get a chance to finish. He wondered if the library might have a copy. He might walk down some afternoon and find out.

During the next three days, Henry continued to observe as small items popped into and out of existence in every room of his house. He was starting to enjoy the visitations, partially because they were so random that they were beyond his power to predict. A pink teddy bear wearing an apron and missing an eye. A DVD set of the complete first season of "Moonlighting." A book on economic theory. A purple sweater, sized for a small woman. A handsaw. A coffee mug that said "World's Greatest Dad." A half-eaten bagel. A live turtle, lumbering slowly across the living room carpet. It hadn't even made it to the tile that formed the border of the kitchen before it vanished.

"I think my house has shifted into some slippery corner of the universe where magic is possible," he emailed to his grandson Mark on the sixth day. "It's strange but wondrous."

Mark wrote back that afternoon. "Sounds intriguing! Come spend Saturday with me and tell me all about it. Carol is taking the girls off on some scouting trip and the house will be quiet. I'll pick you up at 10 if that's OK."

That was always OK. Henry tried not to have favorites, but he preferred Mark out of all his seven grandchildren. He was dark, like Ellen; like her, he had boundless energy and inexhaustible reserves of curiosity. No story too dull, no theory too vast, to catch Mark's full attention.

It was no surprise that the tale of the mysteriously appearing and disappearing objects was instantly intriguing to Mark. "There's no pattern at all?" he inquired as they sat on the couch in Mark's living room. "Food in the kitchen, clothes in the closet, toothpaste in the bathroom?"

Henry shook his head. "None that I've been able to detect."

"Sounds when they appear and disappear? Heat, cold?"

"Don't think so."

"No limits on time of day?"

"Well," said Henry cautiously, "I don't know if any appear in the middle of the night. They might, and I just don't see them."

Mark nodded and seemed to review something in his head. "Are you familiar with the tenets of quantum physics?" he asked.

Henry gave him a look from under his brows. "No."

Mark made motions with his hands, as if his fingers could more gracefully explain concepts that were too intricate for words. "It's difficult to explain, but scientists are pretty sure that at the subatomic level, molecules and portions of molecules really can—well, teleport, essentially. Move from one space to another space without actually traversing the distance. That's the quantum leap you've heard about."

"Like the TV show."

"Right. Well—all right, good enough. So if electrons and protons can make these leaps over short distances, theoretically there's nothing to stop a whole mass of them from making the leap all at one time. Ergo, one complete, solid object could transport itself from one fixed place to another. From my house to yours, say."

"Would they always go back to your house, then?" Henry said. "I mean, so far nothing's stayed very long, but I have no way of knowing if the items are returning to where they came from, or if they're going on to someplace else altogether."

"I don't think science tells us that."

"And why would they come to *me?*" Henry asked.

Mark grinned. "Maybe the universe is sending you a message."

"With turtles and boxes of Cracker Jacks? Pretty obscure message."

"I've never thought of the universe as being particularly easy to decipher," Mark said with a laugh. His face lit up as a new thought crossed his mind. "Do you ever get spam email?"

"Constantly," Henry said dryly.

"For a while I was getting emails with these amazingly creative phrases in the subject line," Mark said. "This is an actual email. I liked it so much I memorized it—'Congolese crayfish abominate powdery henbane emulsion conjecture little stuffy velour aviatrix ditto dichotomous abdomen.' Who would think up something like that? It's the randomly generated poetry of our technologically enabled society, I thought. The next wave of emails consisted of words with numbers attached. Like 452 biennium and 455 infest. I decided it was poetry being delivered one word at a time. The numbers were assembly instructions."

Henry just looked at him. "And what does this have to do with me and my strange little problem?"

Mark waved his expressive hands. "The universe is sending you its own version of poetry. A crazy kind of sonnet."

"Not enough structure for a sonnet," Henry said.

Mark grinned. "Haiku, then. All about balance."

"Free verse, I think, if it's poetry at all."

Mark leaned forward. "But here's another thought. Are the objects coming to you or to your house? Has anything materialized around you when you were somewhere else?"

Henry shrugged. "I don't know. This is the first time I've left the house for any length of time since it started to happen."

Mark leaned back. "That might be your message, then."

"What?"

"That you should leave the house more often. If you don't get out and stroll around the world, the world will find a way to stroll around you."

Henry thought that over. He tried to walk a half mile or more every day. There was a Walgreens on the corner where he could fill his prescriptions and buy a few necessary items, and the local library was right across the street from the store. Who needed more than books and the occasional quart of milk on a daily basis? He generally had groceries delivered, and one of his daughters would come pick him up any time he needed to get to a doctor or do some serious shopping. It was true he had let the parameters of his world shrink down more than he should have. Ellen would never have permitted such a thing to happen.

"Our little neighborhood runs a bus that'll take you down to Seaton Square," Henry said slowly. Seaton Square was about five miles from his house, a pretentious but pretty shopping mall built around a central green space alive with fountains. "Anybody can ride it, but it's mostly seniors and a few young mothers with their babies. If you call before ten in the morning, they'll come right to your door to pick you up."

"Maybe you ought to do that every once in a while," Mark said. "But you know you can call me any time you need a ride. And Mom and Aunt Kelly are only twenty minutes away."

Henry nodded. "Yeah. But I'm gonna try the bus first. That's a good idea, Mark."

Mark opened his mouth to answer, but he was interrupted by the tinny sound of a small synthesizer playing Pachelbel's *Canon*. Mark grinned. "Nice ringtone," he said.

Henry glanced around. Sure enough, there was a small black cell phone lying on the bookcase across the room. Henry was reasonably certain it hadn't been there before. "Not mine," he said.

Mark's eyes lit up. "Quantum leap!" he cried, and he jumped up to run over and get a closer look. But he was only two steps from the bookcase when the cell phone vanished. The *Canon* was still playing.

Monday morning, Henry phoned the folks at the START bus (Seniors Traveling Around "R" Town, which made him chuckle every time he saw the logo). An hour later, he was waiting in front of his house when the perky blue and white van pulled up in front, the logo festooned on almost every available surface. It was a gorgeous day for October, in the low 60s and saturated with sun, and Henry was smiling when he climbed on board.

There was only one other passenger, and he happened to know her: Amanda Borden, who lived three blocks over. She had been in Ellen's gardening group and book club, but she was also a loud voice in local politics, almost always supporting the liberal causes that were unpopular in this conservative district. Amanda was a good ten years younger than Ellen had been and possessed a similar sort of restless energy. She had curly, shoulder-length red hair just now shading over to gray, and a freckled face creased by years of laughter. The instant she saw him, she waved him over.

"Henry Cline! I haven't seen you in months!" she exclaimed as he dropped into the seat across the narrow aisle from her. "How've you been? Feeling all right?"

Ellen had always despised the fact that anyone over the age of sixty started every conversation with a health check, but Henry was actually glad to have someone inquire. Maybe because he liked his answer. "Good. A little trouble with my eyes, so I don't really drive any more, but not too many aches. How about you?"

Amanda gestured down at her foot, which was wrapped in what looked like a walking cast. Henry noticed a sporty black cane resting against her seat. "Oh, I had bunion surgery on my right foot, so I'm not supposed to walk much or drive with it, but I can't stand sitting in the house all day. So I've been taking the bus to the Square every day, having a cup of coffee, and coming home again. Makes me cheerful enough to keep from setting the neighbor's cat on fire."

That made him snort with laughter. "I'm just out for a little variety myself," he said. "Hadn't thought about what I'd do once I got there."

"Well, come have a coffee with me. One of those frappuccinos. You just know they've got to be horrible for you, but I'm seventy. I've been good all my life. I think I'll get it *with* the extra shot of cholesterol, thank you very much."

"I don't know that you've been good all your life," he observed. "Unless you're talking strictly diet."

That elicited a sharp crack of laughter. "I think my ex-husband would say you're right," she agreed.

"So how are your boys? Any news?"

She opened her mouth to answer, but the words were suspended when an orange baseball cap suddenly materialized on Henry's lap. Amanda stared at it a moment, then lifted her eyes to his face. She seemed as intrigued as she was astounded. "Have you been practicing sleight of hand?" she asked. "Because that trick is very good."

Henry felt a faint smile come to his mouth. He lifted up the hat and fitted it on his head. "I'd tell you, but you wouldn't believe me."

"Tell me anyway."

"Things have just started appearing. Hanging around for a few minutes, then disappearing again. I don't know where they come from. I don't know where they go. It's the damnedest thing." He peered at her from under the bill of the cap. "I kind of like it, though."

"I *love* it," she replied breathlessly. "But—these items are real? You can touch them? I could touch them?"

For an answer, he handed over the cap and she put it on her own jaunty curls. "It sure feels real," she said, digging in her purse and coming out with a mirror. "Ew, bad color for me, though. Now, if I had a green hat, I—"

Before she could finish her sentence, the hat had disappeared. Her eyes were huge as they stared back at her reflection, and then over at Henry.

"Told you," he said.

Her face was bright as an Easter sunrise. She exclaimed, "This is the most charming thing that's happened to me for weeks!"

Henry had no other plans for Seaton Square, so he paced slowly alongside Amanda as she hobbled around, leaning on her cane. They looked in shop windows, exclaimed at the prices of the merchandise, shook their heads over what passed for fashion nowadays, and talked, by Henry's strict count, to four thousand strangers who responded happily to Amanda's blinding smile.

"I think I finally understand what people mean when they say things like, 'Oh, Amanda, she's never met a stranger,'" he told her as they sat at the window table of a Starbucks and watched the crowd saunter past.

Amanda laughed. "Well, you know, you can be friendly or you can be grouchy, and it always seems to take less effort to be friendly. Too much work to be mean-spirited."

Henry sipped at the vanilla frappuccino Amanda had insisted he order. He had thought it was too sweet until she told him to think of it as ice cream, and then he liked it a lot. "I don't think of myself as grouchy, exactly, but I find it easier not to be drawn into casual interactions with people I've never met and am unlikely to see again."

"I get a little kick every time anyone smiles at me, even a stranger. Sometimes especially a stranger. Especially a stranger with a dour look on his face. Yes, like that one!" she said. "I like to see if I can win him over."

"How often do you fail?"

She actually stuck her tongue out at him and tossed her red hair. "Not as often as you'd like to think."

They were there long enough to decide that second cups of coffee were in order. Henry fetched them, since Amanda's foot was aching. "Our *barista* is named Tiffany," he told her as he sat down again. He just wanted to say the word *barista,* which he had seen on a sign over the counter. "She seems too young for a name like that. Shouldn't she be a Haley or an Emma instead?"

"And what *about* all those girls named Tiffany?" Amanda demanded. "What happens to them when they're eighty-five? Amanda was a pretty name when I was a teenager, and it's a classic name now that I'm a grandmother. But what happens to all these Tiffanys and Crystals when they get old?"

"Maybe they'll never get old," Henry said.

"Everybody gets old."

He shrugged and gave her a lurking smile. "Lotta magic at work in the universe," he said. "Maybe these girls will be suspended in time. Get the right name when you're born, you never have to age."

Amanda rolled her eyes, but then she seemed to think it over. She sat forward in her chair, her face animated. "Wouldn't that be something," she said. "There's a phrase people use, when they're trying to be sarcastic, when they're trying to belittle something someone else has done. They say, 'Wonders never cease.' But I love that phrase. Think about it! The Grand Canyon. Heart surgery. Land rovers on Mars. They're all amazing. They're all wonders. And there are new wonders being dreamed up every day. So I don't know, maybe you're right. Maybe some magic will come down and touch some people and they'll never get old. That would be pretty awe-inspiring." She gestured with her right hand, as if trying to conjure words out of the air.

Instead, a vase of yellow roses materialized in the middle of the table. There were twelve of them, and they exuded a subtle but insistent scent. Amanda laughed in delight, and then made a great show of leaning forward, closing her eyes, and inhaling deeply. Henry's attention was caught by Tiffany and her fellow *baristas*, who stood slack-jawed behind the serving counter, staring in their direction.

But his gaze went right back to Amanda when she opened her eyes and smiled at him. "As I was saying," she said. "Wonders never cease."

Tuesday, Henry took the START bus to Seaton Square again, accompanied once more by Amanda. This time they ate hot fudge sundaes at a local sweet shop and argued about who should run for mayor. He skipped Wednesday so he could have lunch with Kelly, and Thursday, so he could putter in the yard on an unexpectedly warm day. But on Friday he called for another pickup, and Amanda was on the bus when it arrived.

"When's that foot going to be healed?" he asked as he helped her down the steps at Seaton Square. "Is it getting better?"

She grimaced, less from pain than irritation, he thought. "Better, but slowly," she said. "Can't wait 'til I can drive again. I'll take you on a road trip. Maybe we'll go all the way downtown someday."

It was too cool to walk around for long, so soon they were back in Starbucks, nibbling on biscotti, which Henry didn't like, and drinking latte, which he did. "Good thing my pension check arrived today," he said as he fetched their second lattes. "Man could go broke drinking this stuff."

Amanda took her first sip as she took every first sip, her eyes closed in a sensual swoon. "Oh, but that's good stuff." She took another swallow, then asked, "Any new manifestations at your house since I've seen you last?"

He nodded. "Couple of books. An electric bill. A glass of wine, half-full. A razor, covered with shaving cream. That must have been an interesting morning, I thought. Man's half through shaving his face and he sets the razor down for a second—and it's gone. Where'd it go? Did he knock it off the sink? He goes out into the bedroom and asks his wife, 'Did you take my razor?'"

"Why would I take your stupid razor?" Amanda chimed in. "You're always blaming me when you lose anything."

Henry grinned. "And he goes back to the bathroom, and there it is, just where he left it. He's probably still confused, two days later."

"Anything else?"

"Well, there was a spider in the kitchen yesterday. I squashed it with a paper towel, but when I threw the paper towel away, it was clean. So, I don't know, did the smashed body teleport back to somebody else's house? That would be pretty weird, I think."

"Who killed this bug and didn't wipe it off the wall?" Amanda said, once more slipping into the part of the annoyed woman of the house. "Honestly, don't you kids know how to keep anything clean?"

"Exactly."

"What do you think—" she started to say, and then stopped with a gasp, staring down at the table. A woman's ring was lying right next to her coffee cup. It was white gold or silver, and its ornate filigree setting held a diamond that looked to be half a carat or more. "Henry," she breathed.

"Somebody's going to be missing that awfully fast," he said.

She snatched it up. "It's *mine*. Henry, it's my mother's wedding ring. I lost it more than ten years ago. Henry, where did you find it?"

He was both pleased and troubled, because of course he had had no knowledge of the ring's existence and no way to direct the magic to fetch it. "Don't ask me," he said. "I don't have a clue. Look, Amanda, this stuff never stays around for long. Don't get too attached to it."

"I know, I know," she said. She slipped the ring onto her right hand and began rummaging in her purse with her left hand. All the while she kept staring at the diamond, turning her fingers this way and that. "But just to see it again—after all these years—oh, I can't tell you how happy this makes me."

She pulled a cell phone out of her bag, flipped it open one-handed, and held it in front of her as if it were a magnifying glass. "Is that a camera phone?" Henry inquired.

She nodded. "I'm taking a picture of my hand with the ring on it. I didn't even have that much when I lost it." There was a tiny flare of light, and then Amanda looked up with a smile. She used his name for the fourth time in about thirty seconds. He thought she must like saying it. "Henry, thank you so much. Even just for this glimpse."

He was a little uncomfortable, but he also felt a certain satisfaction at the thought that he had been able to give Amanda such a gift. "Anything to oblige a lady."

She put the phone away and kept studying her hand. "I wanted to use it as my wedding band, but Carter had already bought me a diamond, and I couldn't tell him I didn't like it. I wore my mother's ring on my right hand for years. After I got divorced, for a few years I was too depressed to wear any rings. They just felt wrong on my hands. But then when I finally got over that stupid feeling, this ring was missing. I looked for it everywhere. I even called Carter and accused him of stealing it. Of course he denied it." She shrugged. "Not one of our more civilized conversations."

"Maybe he did steal it," Henry said. "And the magic has stolen it from him. At least for a while."

She wriggled her fingers again. "But it's mine for a moment."

In fact, the ring stayed on Amanda's hand for the rest of the day. They left Starbucks about half an hour later, the ring still in place, and it didn't vanish as they meandered through a gift shop or waited for the START bus to arrive. She was still admiring it during the whole ride home.

"I wonder what the statute of limitations is," Amanda said. "You know, 'If it doesn't disappear within twenty-four hours, it has now solidly made its place in a new reality.' I wonder when I can be sure it's mine to keep."

"I don't know if it works that way," Henry said. He shrugged. "Even life doesn't work that way. You can never count on keeping anything, or anyone, one heartbeat past the present moment."

Amanda sighed, and then, as the bus jolted to a halt in front of Henry's house, she smiled. "A lesson we've all had to learn over and over again," she said. "But thanks for teaching it to me again in such a pretty way."

She waved as he climbed down the steps, waved again as he glanced back from the front door. Once inside the house, he didn't know what to do with himself, and for the rest of the afternoon he proved too restless to settle. So he worked out in the garden for a while, despite the chill, then spent some time cleaning out boxes in the basement. Right before it got dark, he walked down to the library to check out a couple new books, but after he got home, he didn't feel like sitting still and reading them.

The START bus didn't run on weekends, so he wouldn't have a chance to see Amanda again until Monday. He could call her, he supposed, and ask if the ring had disappeared yet, but he didn't know her number. He wondered how long it would stay on her hand before the magic reclaimed it. Or maybe this was the end result of magic; maybe the universe had transported her ring somewhere else for ten long years and only today remembered to return it. He would have to ask Mark if such a thing were possible.

He was sitting over dinner that night, trying to get interested in one of the library books, when a photograph appeared next to his glass of water. He picked it up and studied it for a long time. It was the last picture he'd ever taken of Ellen, two weeks before she had the aneurysm that killed her without warning. She was heading out the door, maybe to meet one of their daughters at the mall, and she was dressed in a bright red sweater. She had paused at the door to wave as she left, and he had snapped the shot to use up the last of a roll of film. Naturally, she was smiling. She looked healthy, she looked cheerful, she looked like she would live for another twenty years.

He had always hated this picture, because it was so obvious that she was saying goodbye. *I'm on my way now. You can't come with me. But don't worry about me, I'm happy. I'm always happy.* He had placed the picture in the bottom of a bag of Ellen's clothes that he donated to some charity, because he couldn't bear to throw it away and he couldn't bear to keep it.

He wondered where it had been all these years, waiting for the right moment to come back to him.

*Goodbye, Henry. I'm on my way now. Be happy.*

He was pretty sure he finally understood what the universe was trying to tell him. A poem, indeed, sprawling and messy though it was. He laid down the photo and went searching for the phone book.

# Can You Hear Me Now?

Stacey was on the phone with her father when he had the heart attack. She heard his gasp, his struggle for breath, the sound of his body falling to the floor. "Dad? Dad? *Dad?*" she cried, but there was no answer except the faraway tinkle of glass breaking three hundred miles away.

They'd both been on their cell phones, because he loved the notion of free long-distance in-network calling. She kept shouting into the cell phone while she leapt across the apartment to dial 911 on the landline. "I have an emergency in another state, I don't know what to do," she panted to the operator who answered. "I can tell you the area code, I can tell you the address—"

The operator was brisk and efficient, and paramedics were on the scene within twenty minutes. But it was too late. Stacey's father had already died.

It was two months after the funeral when the first call came.

The power had been flickering off and on all evening as a thunderstorm blew through the city. A lightning strike that had to have hit the nearest streetlamp was followed by a roll of thunder that actually rattled the furnishings. Seconds later Stacey's cell phone churned out the opening bars of Blondie's "Call Me," the ringtone she'd chosen back in more carefree days. No number came up on caller ID, but that wasn't unusual; three of her friends were lawyers who routinely blocked data on their outgoing lines. Stacey flipped open the phone.

"Hello?"

"Hey, sweetie, how've you been doing this week?"

She dropped to the couch because her legs folded beneath her. "*Dad?* But—how—where—"

"Have you enrolled in that whatchamacallit like you said you would? That matchbox service?" His voice was rough and warm, a little froggy, like he might have caught a cold and was trying to conceal it from her.

Stacey was so confused she hardly knew whether to scream or sob. "I—what? Matchbox? Oh, you mean that online dating thing?"

She remembered now. The last time they'd been talking, right before the heart attack, he'd been quizzing her about her love life. *I don't have a love life, Dad. I haven't met a new guy in two years.* That's when he'd started asking her about computer dating. Had she ever tried that? What did it cost? He'd pay for it if it was too expensive. But she was such a pretty girl, such a nice girl, all a guy would have to do was meet her and he'd want to take her out.

"That's it," he said, sounding pleased. "Did you ever enroll?"

"No, I—I've been busy." *I've been distracted. I arranged your funeral. I attended your funeral. I cleared out your apartment and settled your debts and dealt with your insurance companies, and I grieved. I buried you, and now you're calling me on the phone.* "What's—what's been happening with you?"

"Oh, you know, same-old same-old. Nothing much ever goes on with me."

It was a ghost—she realized it was a ghost, it had to be—but she'd never heard of a ghost that could make phone calls. She figured there was a strong possibility she was dreaming. Or crazy. But once her shock and bewilderment started to fade, she found herself flooded with happiness at the chance to hear his voice again.

"Your health?" she said, pressing a little. *What does it feel like to be a ghost?* "How's your knee?"

"Hasn't bothered me at all lately! And my back's been good, too. I'm having a little trouble remembering things, but I haven't forgotten anything important. Don't you worry."

"I—no, I wasn't worried. I was just—well, it's good to hear from you, that's all."

"So? This dating service? Have you signed up?"

Stacey couldn't restrain a slightly hysterical laugh. Even after death, her father was determined to see her married. She wondered if he planned to call her every week for the rest of her life until she finally tied the knot.

It was enough to make her consider remaining a spinster forever. Though she supposed twenty-seven wasn't old enough to qualify for the word yet.

"I haven't," she said. "A couple days ago I talked to the guy next door, though."

"Guy next door? Who's that?"

She couldn't believe it. Her father was calling from beyond the grave and *this* was the topic they were stuck on. "Um—he said he was Nathan. He moved in about a month ago. He's really cute, but I don't know anything about him. I mean, we talked for five minutes."

"Is he tall? You're a tall girl."

She strangled a laugh. "Yeah. Yeah, he's tall. But Dad, listen, let's talk about you for a minute. What are you—"

"Wait a second, honey." There was a muffled sound, as if he'd put his hand over the receiver, and then he came back on. "Listen, I've got to go. I'll call you later."

"But Dad—"

Then he was gone.

Stacey was so stunned she just sat there for five minutes, staring at the open phone in her hand. *That could not have just happened. Stress has finally warped your brain and you're hallucinating. Time to call a doctor.*

Or call somebody, anyway. She was mentally flipping through her address book, wondering who could offer both a soft pat of sympathy and a sharp dose of reality, when a sudden loud crashing in the hall made her jump to her feet and drop the phone. Running over to throw open the door, she found her neighbor Nathan in the hallway, kneeling on the floor in a welter of spilled groceries. Oranges and melons had rolled down the first two stairs; what looked like ketchup and grape juice made a gooey cocktail on the welcome mat right in front of Nathan's door.

"You want some paper towels?" Stacey asked.

He looked up, his face rueful. Still cute. He had wide cheekbones and a firm chin, hazel eyes and straight brown hair that badly needed cutting. "I was thinking maybe a bath mat. Sop the whole mess up and throw it away."

"I don't have a spare one of those. Oh, but I have a raggedy old beach towel I used to clean up my car when a friend of mine threw up in the back seat."

"Sounds perfect." He glanced at the mess again, his face even more rueful. That's when Stacey realized that the dark purple liquid was not, in fact, grape juice. "I'd offer you a glass of wine for your help but it seems like the wine is one of the items that did not survive the fall." He gestured at his door. "I've got some Jack Daniels left over from a poker game the other night."

She laughed. "Let me get the towel."

It took them half an hour to clean up the mess and retrieve the salvageable foodstuffs. Nathan carried the welcome mat inside his apartment to dump it in the shower, leaving behind a purplish aureole of color around a pristine rectangle on the hall carpet. Stacey brought in the last of the supplies and laid them on the counter that separated the small kitchen from the living room. She couldn't resist taking a quick look around. His apartment was laid out like a mirror image of hers, so she guessed the two rooms she could see in the shadows off the hallway led to a cramped bathroom and a single bedroom. The open living area wasn't exactly spotless, but no worse than her own, with newspapers piled in corners and shoes kicked off beside the battered couch and a humongous plasma TV taking up all the space on the interior wall.

Nathan reappeared, drying his hands on his jeans. "I really appreciate your help. Can I get you something to drink? I just remembered, I've got a couple beers, too, if that sounds better. Or Coke, if you'd rather."

"I just got a phone call from my dad," Stacey said.

Something in the tone of her voice caused him to pause in the act of turning toward the kitchen. His eyebrows lifted. "Is that a good thing or a bad thing?"

"He's been dead for two months."

Nathan nodded and continued on toward the kitchen. "Right, then. Whiskey it is."

They sat on Nathan's couch and talked for the next two hours. Despite looking like a dispirited floor model from a rundown furniture factory, Nathan's fuzzy brown couch was surprisingly comfortable, and the Jack Daniels was smooth as honey. Both of them encouraged Stacey to confide.

"I loved my dad, but he would drive me crazy. He'd call me two or three times a day with something stupid he wanted to tell me. A joke, or the plotline of some made-for-cable movie that didn't make any sense. Sometimes I didn't answer the phone when he'd call because I couldn't fake the interest for another half hour. And then after he died—" She pressed a hand to heart. "I kept thinking, 'Oh, what wouldn't I give for one more call from Dad?' And then tonight. When he *called.* I kept thinking I was hallucinating." She glanced around the apartment. "I still think I might be."

Nathan leaned back. He'd kicked his shoes off and stretched out, slouching down so his head rested on the back of the sofa and his butt was almost off the seat cushion. "Well, *I'm* not hallucinating. I think we're both very real. But I can't explain the phone call. I've never believed in ghosts."

"No, me either!" Stacey leaned forward. "This sounds so weird but—I was talking to him on my cell phone when he had the heart attack. Do you think—would it make sense— I mean, could his soul or his consciousness or whatever have imprinted on my phone? Like, gotten tangled up in its electronics somehow? I mean, when you think about it, how remarkable is it that we can transmit voices three hundred miles? We aren't even sending sound through wires any more. Those voices are going through *air,* from one little handheld device to another. So why can't souls go through the air, too, and end up in a phone?"

Nathan spread his hands. "I can't answer questions like that. I'm not a science guy who can explain electricity and conductivity and fiber optics. And I'm not a religious guy or a New Age guy, so I can't tell you what souls do and how spirits move through the vortex or whatever. I mean, I believe you, but I couldn't tell you why or how it happened."

Stacey took another sip of her whiskey. It was amazing how the alcohol smoothed away all the rough edges. The disembodied call no longer seemed so spooky or unnerving, and the sorrow she had carried around with her for the past eight weeks had loosened its grip on her ribcage. She couldn't imagine why she hadn't been drinking more or less continuously since her father's death. "Well, what kind of guy are you?" she asked.

"Software engineer guy."

Her response was half a laugh and half a hiccup. "Oh, because there's such a need for those here in Kansas City."

"Well, I wanted to get away from Silicon Valley. And … stuff there."

"What kind of stuff?"

"My wife died six months ago."

"Oh, I'm so sorry! That's terrible."

He took another swallow of amber liquid. "We'd been separated for a year. It's a long story."

"You don't have to tell me about it," she said. "But I'd listen if you feel like talking."

He was silent a moment, studying the liquor in his glass, then he shrugged. "We got married just out of college. Had all those early hardscrabble days that you're supposed to remember fondly when you're older and richer. Lived in an apartment smaller than this one with crazy neighbors upstairs and a drug dealer downstairs, or at least that's what we always assumed." He paused again, remembering, or maybe trying to edit the story down to its essentials. "We argued a lot. And it didn't get better once we both had jobs and could afford a bigger place. We just had more rooms to argue in. Finally we agreed to a separation."

He straightened up, poured himself another shot of whiskey, then sat there a moment, resting his forearms on his knees and gazing backward at his past. "We still called each other every week or two, but I knew she was seeing someone else. I tried to go out with other girls but I couldn't really get in the spirit of dating. Then one night she died in a car crash. One of our friends told me she'd been trying to get up the courage to ask for a divorce so she could get married again."

Stacey knocked back the last of her whiskey and held her glass out for more. "Well, that sucks rocks."

Nathan carefully poured another portion into her glass; she could tell he was rationing. He didn't seem miserly, so she figured that meant he realized she was drunker than she realized she was, and he was trying to spare her the effects of excessive inebriation.

"Yeah," he said. "That's what I always thought."

"So you left California to leave your memories behind," she said. "Is it working?"

"Not so far," he said. He looked surprised. "Except. Well. Talking to you tonight. I haven't thought about Mandy until I started telling you the story."

"I know. This is the first time I've felt kind of cheerful since my dad died." She looked at the glass in her hand. "Do you think it's the whiskey?"

He shook his head. "Probably not. I've had whiskey before and it hasn't helped this much. I think it's the company."

"Oh." She thought that over a moment, and then she smiled at him tentatively. "Well, I'll be happy to scare away your ghosts any time you're willing to hear me talk about mine. I don't know—did that sentence make any sense?"

"Enough sense for me to know what you meant," he said. He was smiling too. "Let's have dinner tomorrow night, and see if the magic lasts."

Stacey thought going out on a Wednesday was probably easier than going out on the traditional date nights of Friday or Saturday, but she was still nervous the next day as she looked over her wardrobe. She wanted to appear cute but not overtly sexy. She was literally the girl next door, and if the dinner didn't go well, she didn't want Nathan to mentally roll his eyes every time he encountered her for the next few months. *Oh yeah… there's the chick who was wearing the see-through black-lace blouse when we went to Red Lobster for dinner.* So she picked a soft white sweater with just enough cling, blue jeans, boots, and an art-glass necklace she'd bought at a street fair. She was relieved that she was having a good hair day, plenty of body still left in her shoulder-length brown curls. A quick sweep of the comb, a swift mist of spray, a deep breath, and she was ready.

Nathan was knocking on the stroke of seven. "I figured I had to be on time since I could hardly say I got stuck in traffic," he said with a grin as she opened the door.

She grinned back. "Are you usually late?"

"Well, I wouldn't say *usually.* It's been known to happen."

She angled her head back to study him. She liked that he was taller than she was; many men weren't. "Because you're disorganized, because you lose track of time, or because you think a deadline is more of a suggestion than a commitment?"

Now he was laughing out loud. "Oh, you're the kind of girl who likes to nail things down, are you?"

"Well, I like to understand the operating system."

They were still standing in her doorway, but now he motioned her forward, so she stepped out and locked the door behind them. They headed down the stairs at a leisurely pace. "Mostly it's because I lose track of time," Nathan said. "I'm a pretty organized guy, so I tend not to forget appointments or misjudge how long it will take me to get somewhere. I say, 'OK, I'll work on this project for an hour and then drive to Joe's,' and when I look up again, two hours have passed and I'm officially late." He glanced down at Stacey. "I do *call*, though, when I realize I'm behind. That is, when I have your phone number."

That surprised a ripple of laughter out of her. "Oh, that was subtle, that was smooth!" she exclaimed. They were in the cramped lobby and pushing out through the main door onto the street. The scents and sights of a Midwestern spring instantly surrounded them—new grass, wet dirt, fluttering birds, a random sprinkling of purple and yellow flowers. "I'd be happy to give you my phone number."

"I mean, sometimes it might be impractical for me to just come knock on the door," he explained, touching her lightly on the back to steer her toward a car parked in front of their building. It looked like a Honda with more than a few miles on it—practical, reliable, comfortable, and well put together. Stacey tried not to draw obvious parallels to its owner. "You might be in the shower—"

"In which case I'm not answering the phone *or* the door."

"Or entertaining romantic guests."

"Haven't been a lot of those lately."

"Or in your pajamas."

She smirked at him as he waited for her to settle into the passenger's seat before shutting her door. "Are you trying to find out what I wear to bed?"

He laughed, closed her door, and circled the car to get in. "Well, I've seen what you wear down to the laundry room," he said, starting the engine. "I figured your nighttime attired was a likely variant."

Now she was giggling, but also trying to remember. "Wait—when did you see me doing laundry?"

"Couple weeks after I moved in. I was getting stuff from my storage locker in the basement, so I don't think you saw me." He had pulled easily into traffic. She liked that he seemed to be a careful driver, though not a nervous one. "You had on this green stretchy top and these black—I don't know—leggings or something. And I thought, 'Wow, there's a girl who doesn't give a damn what anyone else thinks of her.'" He glanced over. "I thought that was pretty cool, but I have to say I was *relieved* to see that you had other options in your wardrobe."

Now Stacey was slumped back in her seat, covering her face and strangling a groan. "Oh, my God, and when I think how I agonized over what to wear tonight! If only I'd realized you'd already seen me at my worst."

"Really? That's your worst? Well, that's something else that's good to know."

"My hair was probably a real mess, too, jammed on top of my head with one of those butterfly clips."

"It was," he said. "Looked like you hadn't washed it in a couple of days."

She heaved a dramatic sigh. "See, it's so unfair. Girls have to spend hours doing their hair and putting on makeup and choosing the right outfit, or they look awful. But a guy can show up wearing a wrinkled T-shirt and baggy shorts, not even having combed his hair, and he looks sexy."

"Yeah, I don't think that's really when I look sexy," Nathan said.

She turned her head to gauge the strong profile, the tousled hair. She thought he was probably wrong in his self-assessment. "So when *do* you look sexy?" she asked.

"When I'm in a tuxedo. I look great."

"Really? And how many times have you worn one?"

"Mmmm. Three times. No, four. Been a best man three times and every time I rocked."

Unsaid went the explanation that his fourth outing in a tux had been at his own wedding, or so Stacey assumed.

"Wow, three times as best man?" she said. "I've been a bridesmaid four times, but only maid of honor once. You must be a great friend. Or have a lot of brothers."

"Only one brother, and he's not married yet," Nathan said. "So I guess I'm a great friend."

She would have asked about those friends, except he was already signaling to pull into a parking lot. "I guess we're here," she said. She kept her voice neutral, but part of her was thinking, *Would have been nice to have some input into the decision about where to have dinner.*

But it was hard to be annoyed when he cut the motor and turned to her with a slightly anxious look. "I hope you're OK with Italian food," he said. "The guy I work with is married to a woman who just opened this restaurant, and I think it's struggling a bit, and I thought it would be nice to give them a little extra business on a weeknight."

Right then, she felt her heart melt. *If this guy is for real, I am grabbing him and never letting go,* she thought. "Love it," she said. "Hope you're OK with garlic."

"Love it. Let's go."

They were debating dessert after a truly fabulous meal when Stacey's cell phone rang. She made no move to dig it from her purse, but Nathan gestured. "Go ahead, get it, I don't mind," he said.

"I'll just see who it is," she said, but no data came up on caller ID. She felt a little tingle go down her back as she flipped open the phone. "Hello?"

"Hey, baby," said her father's voice, still a little gruffer than it used to be. "How you doing today?"

"Hi, Dad," she said, and watched Nathan straighten in his chair. "Good. I'm out on a date."

"Yeah?" He sounded pleased. "Who with?"

"The guy in the apartment next door. We got to talking last night and we had a good time, so we decided to go to dinner today." At her words, Nathan nodded emphatically.

"Yeah? Is he nice?"

"Seems to be."

"Good-looking?"

"*I* think so."

"Is he going to pay for the meal?"

She had to choke back a laugh. "We haven't gotten that far yet."

His voice took on a scolding note. "You shouldn't be all modern and insist on splitting the check. A man *likes* to take care of a woman."

"I'll keep that in mind. Hey, Dad, how are *you* doing? How are you feeling?"

"Great, couldn't be better. But I gotta go, honey. I'll call you next week."

He disconnected, and Stacey was left staring at a silent phone. She felt a curious mix of euphoria and unease that left her shaky and off-balance.

"Kind of freaky, huh?" Nathan said in a soothing tone.

Stacey lifted her eyes to gaze at him. He was solid and sincere and as far from spectral as you could get. "Pretty freaky," she agreed. "On the one hand—wow, how great to hear his voice! On the other hand—it's really spooky. I feel kind of—" She let a tremor run down her back. "Shivery."

"Do you think he's going to call you every day?"

She stopped herself right before uttering an automatic *God, I hope not.* "I have no idea," she said. "That would certainly take some getting used to."

He nodded. "Well, there's really only one way to deal with events as unnerving as this." At her inquiring look, he said, "Double chocolate espresso cake."

She laughed, and the shivers went away.

He paid for dinner, too.

Even though the meal had gone so well, Stacey felt herself growing ridiculously tense as they drove back to the apartment and climbed the stairs. She'd never been the type to sleep with a guy on the first date, and there was still that *how-weird-would-it-be-to-live-next-door-to-an-ex* question knocking around inside her head. So the night's goodbye felt uncomfortable to her before they'd even arrived at their adjoining doors.

When she risked a look up at Nathan, he wore a thoughtful expression. "I can't decide if this is cool or awkward," he said. "Pretty easy to walk you home! But kind of strange to just wave and say goodnight."

She relaxed a little. "I keep looking ahead," she confessed. "You know, after we have the torrid affair, then we break up, and then we're always running into each other on the stairwell, and half the time you've got a new girlfriend with you—makes it hard to live in the moment."

He rubbed the back of his neck. "The torrid affair part sounds good, though," he said.

It surprised a laugh out of her. "Yeah, I haven't had torrid in a while."

Before she'd had time to brace for it, he leaned down and kissed her on the cheek. "But maybe we'll hold off on that for a few days," he said. "Till we get to know each other a little better."

She smiled up at him. "That sounds good."

"Not this weekend, though," he said, sounding regretful. "I have to work twelve-to-twelve both days. We're installing a new system and it's supposed to be up and running by Monday. It *won't* be, but the software guys are working around the clock to make it look like we're doing our part to get it going."

"OK, well, I'll blow you a kiss if I see you in the hallway," Stacey said. "Goodnight. Thanks. It was—I really had a great time."

"Me, too."

He stood there and watched her as she fumbled for her keys, which of course were at the very bottom of her purse under her wallet, her sunglasses, her makeup case, her comb. She was blushing when she finally unearthed them and unlocked the door. He was still watching her, so she paused and blew him a kiss before going in. She stood just inside her apartment and waited until she heard his door open and shut before she threw the lock and headed to her bedroom.

It was three in the morning Saturday night—or Sunday morning—when the next call came. Stacey was so disoriented that at first she didn't recognize the tinny, rhythmic music as being the sound of her cell phone ringing in the other room. She dragged herself out of bed, practically knocked over the lamp as she turned it on, and stumbled into the living room, groping for her purse. She was surprised that the phone was still ringing; it usually went to voice mail long before this.

"Hello," she said breathlessly when she finally found it and pried it open. There had been no number listed on Caller ID, so she half-expected to hear her father speaking in reply.

But she didn't. "Hello? Hello? Carina?" asked a woman in a rushed and frantic voice.

"No, wrong number," Stacey said wearily.

"Don't hang up! Please don't hang up!" the woman cried. "I've been trying for days—I can't get through—I don't know what's wrong with her phone—"

Stacey sank to the couch, one hand holding the phone to her ear, one hand shielding her eyes from the lights she'd just turned on. "Maybe you could call the operator to assist you."

"I did! Of course I tried that! But the operator won't answer either. *No one* answers. I've tried every phone number I can think of. You're the first person I've been able to get through to."

Stacey felt a cold premonitory tickle send a live current down her spine. "Where are you calling from? Maybe there's some—cell tower down or something."

"I'm in New York. There are cell towers everywhere! Look, could you take a message for me?"

"I don't know—"

"Please. Call my mom. Tell her I'm fine. I'm working on the story, and it's going great."

"But I—"

"I'll give you her number. Do you have a pen and some paper?"

Stacey figured it would be easier to acquiesce, even if she never made the call. So she found a pencil and an empty envelope from the gas company and dutifully took down the number. "Who should I say you are?"

"Teresa Sanchez," the woman said, and then she laughed. "Well, of course you don't have to tell my *mother* my whole name. Just tell her Teresa called. Oh, and tell her it's a lot warmer than I thought it would be! I don't even need my coat."

That caught Stacey's attention. "You don't—"

But the connection had already been cut.

Stacey sat there a few more minutes, more awake with each passing second, and finally nerved herself to boot up her laptop. She went straight to Google and typed in Teresa Sanchez. And swallowed a squeak of terror when the first page to come up was a two-week-old news item on CNN. com: *Journalist Shot in Central Park.* "A 34-year-old reporter in town to interview a source was found dead early this morning. Police speculate that Teresa Sanchez was killed by a man she had come to talk to as part of a story she was writing for the *San Francisco Chronicle…*"

"Jesus," Stacey whispered, rocking a little as she sat on the couch, the laptop on her knees. "Oh my God. Oh God."

Not even bothering to shut down the computer, she set it on the end table and came to her feet, unsteady enough she thought she might tip over. Her hands were shaking and she was cold to the bone. "Now what?" she said aloud, rubbing her fingers against her thighs. She was wearing an old KU t-shirt and plaid Christmas pajama bottoms; the flannel felt good against her fingertips, but the friction wasn't generating any warmth. "I just go back to bed? What if the phone rings again? Oh God, oh God—"

She shouldn't do it. She scarcely knew him. He'd been working all night, had probably been asleep for barely two hours. But she grabbed her keys and ducked out into the hallway anyway, knocking hard on Nathan's door and standing there shivering until he answered it. He was tall and sleepy and even more rumpled than she was, wearing boxers and an inside-out undershirt.

"I'm sorry—I got another call and it freaked me out—from a stranger this time, and she wants me to phone her mom, but she's *dead*, she was killed in New York City, but I don't think she knows she's dead and I—Nathan, I'm sorry but I—"

That was all the farther she got before he reached out and pulled her against him in a hug. He was warm and solid and smelled like deodorant soap. "Leave your phone in your apartment and come stay here for the night," he said, his sentence split in the middle by a yawn. "No one will bother you."

Stacey woke to the smell of coffee and the feeling of acute embarrassment. She knew exactly where she was—in Nathan's apartment, in Nathan's *bed*—though all they'd shared during the night were the blankets. Well, and a little human contact. He'd tucked her in like a child, then stretched out beside her on the king-size futon that took up almost the entire bedroom. He was far enough away that she could scarcely feel his body heat. But he'd turned on his side, facing her, and taken her hand in a comforting clasp.

"Go to sleep," he said, and instantly dropped off.

Stacey had been unable to comply, at least at first. She'd lain there for a good hour, alternately rigid and trembling, before sheer exhaustion had forced down her eyelids and she'd slept.

And now it was the morning after and she felt like a complete idiot. Nathan would think she was crazy. Would think she was needy. Would think she was selfish and stupid and careless of other people's privacy and heedless of their desire to sleep after a really long workday that she had been told about in advance. And what must she *look* like? She buried her face in the pillow. Maybe she could stay here and pretend to be asleep until he left for his second long shift.

But no. She had to use the bathroom. And she had to be an adult about this, get up, face him, humbly apologize, swear she would never do this again.

Unless she got more scary phone calls in the night, but she refused to think about that right now.

She was able to get to the bathroom without him seeing her and uttered a muffled cry of dismay when she saw herself in the mirror. Hair a mass of tangles, face pale and puffy, sleeping ensemble too wretched to contemplate. She used hand soap to wash her face, her index finger and Nathan's toothpaste to clean her teeth, and a comb she found in the medicine cabinet to improve her hair, if only by a narrow margin. She took a deep breath and headed toward the kitchen where Nathan appeared to be making breakfast. He stood at the stove, his back to her; by the wonderful smell, she thought he was frying bacon and eggs.

For a moment, she studied what she could see of him. He'd thrown on a robe but didn't seem to have bothered with the comb. His body language was relaxed. In fact, she thought he might be humming.

She took another deep breath and said, "I am so, so sorry. I should never have come over and woken you up in the middle of the night—"

He'd turned at her very first words, a smile already on his face. "Not a problem," he said. "I'm glad I was here."

Nathan had to leave by 11:30, so Stacey called Teresa's mother at 11, because she wanted him there for moral support if it all went badly. She sat on the fuzzy brown couch, while he settled in to the nearby chair, looking at ease as always.

The 510 area code must be in California, Stacey thought; she wasn't surprised when the woman who answered had a strong Spanish accent. "Good morning, you don't know me, but I'm calling about your daughter, Teresa," Stacey said.

She heard the gasp on the other end. "Teresa? Sí? Are you with the police?"

"No, no—this is very strange, so I want you to hear me out instead of hanging up, OK? My father died a few months ago, but lately his—his spirit has been contacting me. Calling me. And last night your daughter called me."

"What? My daughter called you?" The incredulous words were followed by a spate of incomprehensible Spanish. Stacey tried twice to interrupt, but a few moments later, a new voice came on the phone.

"This is Diego, I'm Teresa's brother," he said in a voice that sounded faintly menacing, even over about fifteen hundred miles of open line. "What are you saying to my mother?"

"Listen. I don't understand it. I didn't ask for it to happen. But I've started getting phone calls from people who are dead." Stacey heard the words coming out of her mouth and almost wanted to laugh. Unbelievable. She would have hung up on anyone who called *her* with such nonsense. She glanced at Nathan and he gave her a reassuring smile and a thumb's up. She continued, "Your sister called last night and asked me to get in touch with your mother. She wanted me to say that she was doing well, she was working on the story. She said she was so warm she didn't even have to wear her coat."

There was a moment's silence. "She was worried about her coat," Diego said. "She didn't have a heavy one to bring with her, you know? She had this green suede jacket, she kept saying, 'Do you think it will be warm enough?' I said, 'It's New York City, you can buy a coat,' but she thought it would be too expensive." There was a sound as if he was shaking his head. "But she didn't have time to shop. She was only there a day before she died."

"I'm so sorry," Stacey said.

"So she called you? Why did she call *you?* Why didn't she call *me?*"

"I don't know. But the past few days I've started getting calls on my cell. See, my dad and I were talking on cell phones when *he* died, and I keep thinking—I don't know— maybe that opened up some conduit to the otherworld or something—"

"Teresa was on her cell phone when she was shot," Diego said sharply. "She was talking to her editor. He heard the gunfire. He heard Teresa scream."

"Jesus," Stacey whispered.

"But you say she's OK now?" Diego asked, sounding for the first time like he accepted the news, like the news was *good.* "She's happy? She's not in any pain?"

"She said she was fine. She said she was warm. She sounded happy."

"*Bueno,*" he said. "*Gracias.* You did a good thing to call *mi madre.*"

"You're welcome," she said. Diego hung up before she could think of another thing to say.

Stacey closed the phone and stared at Nathan. "I think he actually believed me," she said.

He shrugged. "Good, since it's true."

"But *is* it? I mean, why do *you* believe me? If you were the one telling me you were hearing from ghosts—well—I wouldn't be going out to dinner with you and letting you in during the middle of the night. I'd be calling the cops and reporting you as a lunatic."

He tilted his head, considering her as if he was considering the question at the same time. "I don't know," he said at last. "I just do."

She took a shuddery breath. "And thank God you do. I'm not quite sure how I'd have gotten through this week without you."

"You realize this won't be the last one," he said.

"The last what?"

"Phone call. You realize if you really do have some—some—conduit to the afterlife, you're going to get more calls."

She could feel her mouth go slack as her eyes went wide. "Hell. Will all of them be people who were on their cell phones when they died?"

Nathan looked interested. "Was Teresa Sanchez?"

"That's what her brother said. And my dad was."

"Well, that narrows the pool to a finite number," Nathan said. "Though not necessarily a small one."

Stacey groaned and put a hand to her forehead. "I think I need some coffee."

"Coming right up," Nathan said, getting to his feet. He paused to glance down at her. "And then maybe—a shower."

She was laughing so hard she couldn't aim straight; the pillow she threw at him landed a good three feet wide. That didn't matter. What mattered was that the laughter loosened some of the dread that had clamped around her heart. But maybe he was wrong. Maybe the phone wouldn't ring again.

Stacey got eight more calls on her cell phone in the next two weeks.

One was from a mountaineer who had just completed a dangerous ascent. "We made the summit, but there was an avalanche as I was calling my wife. Could you let her know it will be a while before we dig out? But it's beautiful here. You cannot believe the view. I've never seen anything like it, not from Everest, not from K2."

Two were from girls who had been in car crashes, one of them rear-ended while she was on the phone with her boyfriend, one having lost control of her vehicle when she tried to text and drive.

Another caller was a man who had been electrocuted while he was trying to fix a wiring problem in his house. He'd been on the phone with his brother, getting instructions that were obviously incomplete. Another was a farmer who slowly bled out in a field two miles from his house after he got his arm tangled in a piece of equipment.

A day later she heard from a young man shot during what was clearly a drug deal. Stacey was nervous about phoning his mother, but this was the one person who readily accepted what Stacey had to say. "He was a good boy," the woman repeated over and over. "He was a good boy. He's in a better place now, with better friends."

She was contacted by a woman who wanted to let the police know someone had broken into her house and she was hiding in the bedroom closet. That was the call that made Stacey sick to her stomach, but the woman herself sounded remarkably cheerful.

"Guess it was just the cat knocking something over in the kitchen," she said. "But I'm going to wait until tomorrow to go down and clean it up. You have no idea how comfortable a walk-in closet is! And it smells so good. I've been using this organic laundry detergent, and all the clothes smell like orange blossom. I think I'm going to start sleeping in here every night!"

The strangest call came from a woman who had dialed a number as she went skydiving for the first time. Stacey could only guess that the woman's chute had failed to open. "I'm trying to tell my friends that I did it," she complained to Stacey. "But no one will answer their phones. I'm 70 years old and I jumped out of an airplane! How cool is that?"

"Pretty cool," Stacey said. "I hope I'm as brave as you are when I'm your age."

She stopped being frightened every time the phone rang. She stopped needing to run to Nathan's when the calls came in the night, though she invariably told him about them the next day, since he invariably stopped by to ask. But the sad, hopeful, confused communications took their toll on her, and she wished they would stop. She ordered a sleek new BlackBerry with a brand-new number, though she didn't trade in the old phone. But she no longer recharged it; she even took the battery pack out.

Even so, the calls still came in, and she still felt obliged to answer them. And obliged to take down messages and contact loved ones and pass on the implausible, inconceivable, and desperately welcome news. *I talked to him this morning and he was at peace… She told me all the pain is gone… It's sunny there, it's safe, no need to be afraid…*

Her father phoned every few days, too. Those calls were more welcome, but wearying in their way. It was hard to entirely let go, to complete her mourning process, when he still seemed so alive and so interested in her life.

He always asked about Nathan. "So? You still seeing that kid next door?"

"He's hardly a kid, Dad. He's thirty-two."

"Why isn't he married if he's thirty-two?"

"He *was* married. It didn't work out."

"Well, you know, maybe he learned how to be a better man to his next wife. Of course, maybe she left him because he's a lazy slob. You want to make sure you find out before you get too attached to him."

"He doesn't seem lazy. Or slobby, either."

"What, you've been inside his apartment?"

*I spent the night there once.* "Sure. I've gotten a glimpse now and then. He seems neat enough."

"I hope he's not too neat. That means he's kind of a funny guy, if you know what I mean."

She couldn't help laughing. "He's just the right level of neat, Dad, but thanks for explaining it to me."

She told Nathan about those conversations, too. During those two weeks, it seemed like she told him everything. What her ghostly callers had said. What her boss had done. What she'd had for lunch. What she'd majored in when she was in college. What she liked about the small Missouri town where she'd grown up. Everything.

His default mode was to listen rather than speak, but any time she prodded him with questions, he willingly answered. When he was a boy, he'd wanted to be a race-car driver. He rarely followed series television, but he could spend hours watching ESPN. The place he most wanted to visit was Alaska, followed by Norway. ("I want to see those Northern Lights.") When he bought his own house, the first thing he was going to get was a dog. ("Big one. Collie or shepherd or Lab. Maybe I'll get two.")

She could tell he liked her. She could see him watching her from time to time with that *look* she remembered from boyfriends in the past—the *look* that meant she was under his skin, on his mind. Occasionally, he'd take her hand or put his arm around her shoulder, but he hadn't kissed her, even on the cheek, since that first date. She thought he was ready to fall in love again, but something was holding him back. It wasn't too hard to guess what that something was.

They'd known each other almost a month when she deliberately brought up Mandy's name. They were sitting in his apartment, having just finished an entire pepperoni pizza that was supposed to feed four, and he'd said, "I think you're the easiest person to be with that I've ever met."

"Glad to hear it," she said. "I always got the idea that Mandy *wasn't* so easy. I have to say I'm a little curious about her. About the two of you."

"Yeah, I can see why you would be," he said. He thought it over for a moment. "Where we were good together," he said, "was in our energy. We both liked *doing* things—riding our bikes, rehabbing the house, doing an Outward Bound course. It was when we had to sit in a room and have a conversation that we started wearing on each other. Picking at each other. Finding faults."

Stacey raised her eyebrows. "Seems like there have to be a lot of conversations between two people who want to live together."

He nodded. "Yeah. If you can't get that right, you're already in trouble." He glanced at her. "That's one of the reasons I think you're so great. I can talk to you."

She felt her heart bound with excitement, but managed to respond coolly, even with a touch of warning. "Yeah, but I'm not a great doer. I don't ride bikes or go hiking through the mountains or play sand volleyball."

"Well," he said with a little smile, "not *yet*."

She smiled back, but briefly. She didn't think they were quite done with the topic of Mandy yet. "So it's been six months since she died—"

"Almost seven by now."

"And you'd been separated a while before the car accident. Where do you feel like you are in the grieving cycle? You know, rage, denial, bargaining, depression, acceptance?"

As always, he seemed to give serious consideration to her question. "I think the rage and denial burned out pretty quickly, but I spent a long time bouncing between bargaining and depression," he said. "I wish I could say I'm at acceptance, but I still keep thinking— If I'd had a chance to hear it from *her*, hear her *tell* me that she was going to marry this other guy—I think that would have made it more real for me, you know? I'd have found it a lot easier to let go."

Stacey nodded. "Makes sense to me."

They were sprawled on his fuzzy brown couch, but now he sat up with a brisk energy. "And I keep wondering—why doesn't *she* call? Why doesn't *she* leave somebody a message?"

For a moment, Stacey was bewildered. "Mandy? You want her to call you?" And then she realized. "You want her to call *me*."

He nodded. "I never mentioned it, but she was on her cell phone when she died. She and her boyfriend were driving to a party, and Mandy was texting one of her girlfriends when he took a turn too fast and went over an embankment. They were both killed."

He gave Stacey a look filled with such pain that she couldn't keep herself from reaching out and taking his hand. "I'm so sorry," she said.

"She was on her cell phone," he repeated. "Why hasn't she called?"

If there was ever a crucial time to give the right answer, it was now. If there was ever a way to help him get over his wife, this was it. Stacey said, "Maybe we could call her. Do you remember her number?"

He looked startled enough to dissipate some of the grief. "But—would that work?"

"I don't know. Worth a try, don't you think?"

For a moment, his grip on her hand clamped tight enough to cause a spasm of pain, and then he released her. "Worth a try."

Stacey retrieved the phone from her purse and handed it over, absurdly glad to see he had to pull out his own cell and check the list of contacts before punching in the number. When he hit the speaker button, she said, "You don't have to do that."

"I want to," he said.

They heard three rings—enough time for Stacey to wonder if the number had been reassigned—before a woman answered with a cheery greeting. Nathan's quick, hard intake of breath was all she needed to be sure this was his wife on the other end.

His voice was a lot steadier than Stacey thought her own would have been. "Hey, Mandy," he said. "I've been thinking about you."

"Nathan!" Mandy replied with unmistakable delight. "How've you been? God, it's great to hear your voice. It's been too long."

"It has been," he agreed. "I'm good. Took a job in Kansas City a few months ago, working with a startup software company—"

"You're in the Midwest? No beaches, no mountains? That's hard to believe!"

"I know. But I like it. Lot of friendly people." He attempted to smile at Stacey, but she could see that his eyes were watering. She gave an encouraging nod in response.

"Well, you always were a people person," Mandy said.

"What about you? Anything new in your life?"

"Oh—Nate—I've been thinking I need to call you. I want to tell you something, but I can't bring myself to say the words."

Stacey saw Nathan swallow hard, as if clearing an obstruction from his throat. "What is it? You can tell me anything."

"You know I've been seeing someone for a while. Greg. He's really a good guy, we get along so well—Nate, we *never* argue, can you believe it? And I argue with everyone."

"That's the truth."

"And the other day—he said—he asked me to marry him. And I want to do it, Nathan. I want to marry him."

"Then I think you should do it."

Stacey thought Mandy might be crying, too. "Really? You're OK with that?"

"I'm OK with it," Nathan said. "I want you to be happy."

Now there was no doubt that Mandy was weeping. "And *you.* I want *you* to be happy. I love you, Nathan. I just—we just—we couldn't get it right."

"I love you too, Mand. Maybe we'll both get it right next time."

"Promise me you will. Promise me you'll start looking for a nice girl." Mandy sniffed and attempted a laugh. "Maybe one of those corn-fed farmer's daughters they seem to grow there in the Midwest. Maybe you could find one of those."

Nathan reached for Stacey's hand again, interlacing his fingers with hers. "Already working on it," he said.

"Good," Mandy said, her voice growing faint. "Listen, Nathan, I've got to go. I'm so glad you called. I feel better about everything."

"So do I. Bye, Mandy."

"Love you! Bye!"

Stacey barely waited until he'd snapped the phone shut before she flung herself across the short distance separating them. She kissed him, she wrapped her arms around his head; she kissed him again. She didn't know if she was comforting him or claiming him, chasing away his ghosts or asking to be let in. Maybe all of those things. It didn't really matter. The only thing that mattered was that his arms curled around her, too; he was kissing her back. He was holding on to her as tightly as she was holding on to him.

She only got one more call on the old cell phone. It came the morning after the first night she and Nathan made love.

"You say you're not much of a doer, but you do that pretty well," had been his judicious assessment, and she had giggled so long that she'd thought she might never fall asleep. She was still feeling pretty upbeat when she was back in her own apartment the next day, and she answered the phone with a breezy hello.

"Well, *you* sound happy," her dad said.

"I am. I had a wonderful date last night—with Nathan, thank you very much—and I'm feeling really optimistic about the long-term chances for this relationship."

"So you love him?"

"It's early days, so it's hard to be sure, but—I think I do."

"That's awfully good to hear," he said. "That's all I wanted to know."

"So how are you doing?" she asked, but there was only empty static on the line. "Dad? Dad?"

Feeling a little unnerved, she shut the phone and set it on the end table, so she'd be sure to hear it if it rang again. But it never did. Not that day, not that week, not that month.

Not ever. Stacey imagined her father hanging up on his end of the line, satisfied and smiling. Once his spirit stopped animating the phone, all the magic was gone from that enchanted artifact; no other calls could come through.

Or maybe it wasn't magic. Maybe it was longing, pure and primal, that had opened and sustained this mystic portal for the past few weeks. It was love, after all, that powered so many miracles, that made possible superhuman feats of strength and will. Stacey knew her father's love was what had caused him to cling to her, worry over her, haunt her, long after he should have moved on. She thought that knowing she had found another kind of love must have given him the strength to let her go.

# THE DOUBLE-EDGED SWORD

I sat at the back of the dark tavern at the table that, in the past five years, had come to be known as mine. Even on the days when I did not bother to leave my house or leave my bed, no one sat in this booth except me. The townspeople knew better, and strangers who made the mistake of sitting in my place would be told politely by Samuel that the table was reserved. I was the only one who ever sat there, and Samuel was the only one who would approach me while I was in possession.

I idly shuffled my zafo cards and began laying out an unspecified fortune. It would be my own, of course; these days, I did not read for anyone except myself. And even then, I was rarely satisfied with the pictures I saw in the cards.

The swinging door to the back room swept open wide, admitting the appetizing smell of meat and onions as well as Samuel's tall, spare figure. Catching sight of me in the dim corner, he checked abruptly and came my way.

"Aesara. I didn't know you were here," he said. "What will you have to drink?"

"Wine, maybe. Do you have time to drink it with me?"

"In an hour or so, I will."

"A glass of ale, then, until you are free," I said.

"Will you eat with me?" he asked.

I squinted up at him in the insufficient light. I had not been awake more than an hour and could not have said with any certainty what time it had been when I rose. "Is it almost dinnertime?" I asked.

"For you, it is," he said firmly. I laughed out loud. Samuel was convinced that I never ate unless he fed me. "Of course, I'm always hungry," he added with a smile.

This was meant to coax me to eat, for his sake. "I'll eat with you," I said. "It smells good."

"I'll get your ale, then."

He disappeared, returning in a minute with a glass of cold ale and a plate of bread. The bread made me laugh again. He grinned crookedly. He was sandy-haired and freckle-faced, with weathered skin and an unchanging ruddy coloring that made it hard to place his exact age. I knew it, though. He was fifty-eight, seven years older than I was, and he had been a widower for five years.

I had laid my zafo cards out in the standard grid—one card in the top row, four cards in each of the next two rows, and a single card in the bottom row—but I had not turned them face-up yet. Now, with the ale and bread arrived as a diversion, I did not feel like reading the cards after all. I swept them back into a pile, reshuffled the deck, and laid the cards aside.

The activity of the tavern went on quietly around me. I leaned back on my padded bench and watched. Although I talked to no one except Samuel, I knew all the employees and all the habitués by name. Sam's eldest son Groyce handled most of the up-front business: greeting customers, making sure everyone was attended, watching out for trouble. Groyce's wife, a small pretty girl, waited on tables and flirted mildly with the local patrons. Two other young women served customers, and an old man cooked in the back.

At this early hour, there were only half a dozen people in the bar, talking quietly, playing board games, or teasing the young girls. I had lived in Salla City for five years now, and I could tell you the name of every man and woman who inhabited it, but I had yet to get closer to a single one of them than I was at this exact moment.

Except for Samuel, of course, and we were only close because of the bargain we had struck one night five years ago. At that, it was not true friendship. He felt grateful and I felt secure; and so he let me stay, and I stayed.

I sipped at my ale and watched Samuel confer briefly with Groyce before disappearing again into the back room. This was the table I had taken that night five years ago, when I had just paused in Salla City to break my aimless journey for one night. Samuel had served me then, but absently, with clumsy, choppy motions that irritated me because some of the wine had spilled from his unsteady hands to the table. I was laying out the cards then, too, and I had been afraid of staining one of them—although it didn't matter if the whole deck was ruined, if the whole deck was lost.

"Could you bring me a cloth, please," I had said coldly, "so I can wipe this up?"

He had immediately done so; but instead of handing me the linen, he had stood beside me wrapping the white napkin around and around his hands.

"You are a *halana*," he said, when I finally looked up with a scowl.

"Yes," I snapped. "What of it?"

"I have—my wife is next door. She is dying. That is—we have a *halana* in the city who has done what she can. She says my wife is dying."

Anger and fear had risen in me, for I knew what was coming next. Knew, and did not want to deal with it. "She is probably right, then," I said.

"But you are a *halana*," he said almost stupidly.

*Halana.* Wise woman; healer. We have varied powers, we who are filled with the magical blood of Leith and Egeva. Some of us are very skilled and some of us are merely well-taught, and I had no way of knowing just how good the local practitioner was.

"There is nothing I can do for you," I said.

He went on as if I had not spoken. "She is in such pain. Her head—her lungs—her whole body. She has begged me to take her life because she is in such terrible agony. But I can't do that."

I wanted to put my hands over my ears and shut out the sound of his voice; I also wanted to put them over my eyes to block out the sight of his face. I could not do both.

"There is nothing I can do for you," I said again. In the six years that I had been wandering through Sorretis—from the throne room of Verallis to the rocky hills of Limbeth— this was the response I had given to everyone who had asked a favor of me. There had not been many. I did not look, with my grim face and darkling expression, like a woman of kindly disposition.

"But she is dying," he said.

I opened my mouth to refuse him again, but somehow the words went unsaid. Perhaps it was the dazed grief in his gray eyes, or perhaps it was the dormant power in my own body that made me say what I had no intention of saying. "I will look at her," I said, rising. "But I make no guarantees. I doubt if there is anything I can do."

And so I accompanied him to the small house behind the big tavern, the house that, under other circumstances, would have been pervaded with a welcoming charm. But a woman lay dying inside, and so the house was filled with fear instead.

I knew as soon as I entered the sickroom that the woman was ill beyond my powers of healing. The chamber was shallowly lit by clusters of tapers shielded behind brightly-painted screens. Someone had brought in fresh flowers in an attempt to cheer up the sick woman; everywhere were similar evidences of hopeful affection. But there were not enough flowers or candles in Sorretis to bring this woman back to life.

I did not say so, of course. She was conscious, but barely; she turned uneasily when I entered the room. "Sam?" she said faintly, and the lanky man crossed to her side. He took her hand so gently he could have been imprisoning butter-flies. Nonetheless, she had to bite back a cry of pain. The look upon his face was sheer desolation.

"I've brought a *halana* to look at you, Mari," he said, in a low voice. I supposed her fever had made her ears sensitive to sound as well. "Can you say hello?"

"*Halana?*" she said drowsily and turned her eyes blindly my way. But I could see from the cloudy irises that she could not make out my features—nor, if it came to that, her hus-band's. I crossed the room quietly and held my hands on either side of her face. I did not quite touch her skin, and she did not moan aloud. Even without touching her, I could feel the heat from her cheeks burn against my palms.

I stayed in the room a few moments, trying to determine what her disease was, while Samuel talked nonsense to dis-tract her. A few minutes was all I could stand; I left as soon as I could have been expected to make a diagnosis. Samuel followed me shortly. On his face was a look of fugitive hope.

"Well?" he said. "Do you think—what do you think?"

I was wont to be blunt at times like these, but he looked so vulnerable that I tried to temper my words. "There are some diseases that can be cured, and some that cannot," I said. "Hers is an illness for which there is no remedy."

He stared at me steadily, while all the light seemed to die slowly from his plain, good-natured face. I had not meant to add even this much, but his expression of despair moved me more than I wished. "I have something I can give her that will ease her pain," I said. "It will not make her well, but it will make her dying less terrible."

"You are sure she will die?"

"In less than a week. Yes, I am sure."

He had flinched when I named the time, but I saw no reason to spare him from the knowledge. "But you can lessen her suffering? With some potion?"

It was not a potion, exactly. I would speak a complex spell over a simple glass of water, and its very essence would change. But I did not explain this to him. Those who are not *halani* prefer to believe in philtres and potions. It makes them uneasy to rely upon incantations. "That is exactly it," I said. "Wait here, and I will return with the drug."

And so I had gone to the bar and requested water, and paused a moment to pour it into one of the small glass vials I always carried. Shortly thereafter, the medicine had been administered. I had not stayed to see the efficacy of my drug. I was hungry, and I had gone back to the tavern to eat my interrupted meal.

Sam had rejoined me in something less than an hour, his face transformed with wonder. Mari was lucid, she who had been raving before. She had allowed him to take her hand, to kiss her face, without crying out from the agony his lightest touch inflicted. He had told her that she was dying, that this blessed surcease was a gift but not the greatest gift, and even so she had laughed. "I feel so good," Mari had exclaimed. "Even the gift of my life could not make me so happy." Sam related this whole conversation to me.

"I am glad to hear it," I had said somewhat sourly, trying to finish my meal.

"How can I thank you?" he demanded. "Such a wondrous thing you've done—"

"I have not saved her," I warned him. "Don't be deceived. Her body is careening headlong toward death, and I can do nothing to arrest that journey."

He watched me steadily again with those gray eyes. I thought somewhat irrelevantly that this man was nobody's fool. "I understand that," he said almost patiently. "But *you* don't understand. She was in such pain and now she is at peace. There is nothing I would not do to thank you."

"Let me finish my dinner in solitude," I said. "And tell no one what I have done for you tonight."

"But—"

"No one," I interrupted. "If you want to thank me, leave me alone. I am not much interested in interfering in the lives of others. And I do not want them interfering in mine."

He had continued to watch me with that narrowed, intelligent gaze, and I had the sudden feeling that I had told him, in a few simple sentences, the whole story of my tangled life. But all he said was, "I understand. I will say nothing to anyone. You will be free from importunity as long as you stay."

Mari had died six nights later. I did not attend the funeral services; Samuel did not ask me to. He did not ask me how long I planned to stay in Salla City. He never asked me to intercede for the life or health of any other citizen, and I was relatively certain that he knew of others, over the years, who could have used my help. He did ask me, the day after Mari died, what my name was. *Aesara,* I said. If he recognized it, he gave no sign.

Samuel himself brought two steaming plates of food to the table about an hour later. Groyce's pretty wife followed with a bottle of wine and two glasses. She smiled at me shyly but said nothing, and fled as soon as she had set the pieces upon the table. Samuel decanted and poured.

"She's afraid of me," I observed.

He looked after his daughter-in-law. "Who, Lina? She thinks you're a crazy old woman. Everyone does."

"I'm not that old," I said.

"But crazy?"

I shrugged. "Who isn't?"

The food was delicious, as always. After Lina had cleared our dishes away, Sam leaned back and stretched his arms. Out of habit, I pulled out my zafo cards again and began shuffling. Sam and I never talked much during meals or after them, but our silences were filled with a wordless companionship.

Now he spoke, surprising me. "Do you ever look at them?" he said.

I glanced up. "What?"

He gestured to the cards that I had laid out again, absent-mindedly, in the standard grid. "Your cards. You always place them on the table this way, but you never turn them over and look at them."

I made a wry face. "Sometimes I do. I don't like the pictures I see."

"What pictures do you see?"

"What pictures does one ever see in a zafo deck?"

"I don't know. I've never seen one."

Now I was amused. "You've never had your fortune told? Not even once, just for fun?"

"No, never. I have too much respect for the powers of the *halani* to approach one lightly."

"Now you do, perhaps," I scoffed. "Since you have such high respect for me."

He grinned. "So do you want to read my fortune?"

I shook my head. "I never read for anyone but myself."

He motioned at the cards again. "Then read one for yourself. I would like to see the pictures."

I hesitated a moment. He caught my reluctance. "Then don't," he said swiftly.

I shrugged and smiled. "Why not? They can't tell me anything I don't know already. But if you have never seen this done, I will have to explain everything."

I turned over the top card, alone in the upper row. "This is called the primary significator," I told him. "It represents me as I am or as I was."

No surprise, the top card was the black queen. I was dark-eyed and dark-haired, but the card meant more than that; it spoke of a somber personality weighted with heavy cares. The brooding queen invariably turned up in my fortune, either as my present or my future.

"Now, most *halani* read the cards in the order in which they are laid out, but I like to skip around," I told him, reaching for the last card, the single one in the fourth row. "This card will tell us who I will become."

The image revealed was not one I was expecting. It was the hooded figure, a dark, faceless form with its hands outstretched.

"It looks somewhat threatening," Samuel observed.

"Indeed. This card means many things, most of them ominous. It stands for the shadowed future, the as-yet-to-be-revealed. Sometimes it is an intimation of death. At other times, it is a warning of a change to come." I gave Sam a twisted smile. "I told you I do not much care for the readings I do."

"You do not have to go on, then," he said seriously.

"No, now I am curious."

I indicated the four cards in the second row. "Fortune, home, heart, career," I recited. "The pictures of my past."

I turned over the cards in order. Fortune: the open box, everything the soul could desire. Home: the lord's castle, with its white stone walls and graceful gables. Heart…but here my own heart nearly stopped beating. The black king, reversed.

"What does it mean when a card is upside down?" Sam wanted to know.

"It means the opposite of whatever the card usually means," I said through a constricted throat. "Or that something has gone wrong with—that person or that thing—"

The last card in this row was scarcely any more comfort. Career: the spilled wine. Promise gone awry…

"None of this makes any sense to me," Sam said.

Perhaps it would not seem so terrible said aloud. "The cards say that at one time I lived a grand life, in a grand house, and my every wish was indulged," I said. "I cared for a dark-haired man but he—something happened to him. And my career from that point on became something of a waste."

He lifted his eyes to my face, his eyebrows raised, but he did not ask me if any of this was true. "And what about your future?"

I was more cautious this time, and turned the cards over one at a time. "Fortune," I murmured. "The double-edged sword. What I have is equally likely to be used for good or for evil. Home." I smiled. "The roadside tavern. Any place of well-being or cheer."

Sam was pleased. "My bar is in your cards?"

"It looks that way." I turned over the third card: the battling twins. "Interesting."

"What? What does that mean?"

"My heart is in conflict. My dreads and my desires pull me in two."

He was watching me again, as if trying to assess the truth of that. "I suppose you know whether or not any of this has any relevance to you," he remarked.

I laughed shortly. "I suppose I do." I turned over the last card. "Career," I named it. "The white queen. It seems a fair-haired woman, or a very good woman, is going to become my patron."

Now Sam was smiling. "That does not seem too likely, at least," he said.

"No," I replied.

Just then the front door opened, and a phalanx of uniformed guards strode in, their feet making a rhythmic tattoo on the wooden floor. It was late spring, and cold, and they wore fur-edged cloaks over their blue-and-gold livery. Behind them, her silk-white hair haloed by the low afternoon sun, entered a small blond woman with an unmistakably noble face. Everyone in the bar stared at her during the few minutes it took her eyes to adjust to the dimness inside. After my first quick look, I turned my eyes back to the table and pushed all my cards together. I knew even before I heard her hesitant footsteps crossing the floor that she had come to Salla City looking for me.

She wanted to speak to me privately, but I insisted that Sam stay to hear our conference. "Whatever you tell me, I will repeat to him," I said listlessly. "He may as well hear everything as you say it."

So Sam moved to my side of the table, and the stranger seated herself across from us, and her five guards arranged themselves as a screen between us and the rest of the tavern. Groyce brought a fresh bottle and a third glass, and Sam poured for us all.

She just touched her lips to the amber liquid and laid the glass aside. "I know who you are," she said.

I felt Sam physically restrain himself from looking at me. He thought I would ask him to leave now, but why should I? He had not betrayed me in the five years he had known me. No matter what was revealed now, it seemed unlikely he would repeat it to anyone.

"How did you find me?" I wanted to know.

She was not ready to drop the discussion of my identity. "Aesara Vega," she said, as if it was a challenge. "*Halana rex.*"

The king's *halana.* I closed my eyes briefly. "Former *halana rex,*" I corrected, looking at her again. She was very beautiful. She had pale skin over delicate bones; her eyes were a flawless blue. On every finger of her left hand, she wore a ring that looked impossibly expensive. On her right hand, she wore only two rings, but neither of them looked cheap, either. "How did you find me?" I asked again.

"Someone who had been in Verallis passed through here several months ago," the woman said. "She recognized you."

It had been eleven years since I had lived at the king's palace in Verallis, and I had changed since then. Whoever had recognized me must have had very sharp eyesight. "I can only suppose," I said quite dryly, "that you have come to me because you need a favor."

"It is a terrible favor to ask," she said. Her voice was low and sweet, and she pitched it most persuasively. The blue eyes looked dense with sadness. I braced myself for what she was going to say, because I knew what it would be, and I was right.

"I want you to kill a man," she said.

I heard Sam inhale sharply. I glanced over at him and smiled. He was trying hard to keep his face under control, but her words had undoubtedly shocked him. "She asks me this," I explained kindly, "because it is believed that I once killed a man in Verallis."

"The king," she said.

Her name, she told us, was Leonora Kessington. Her husband was Sir Errol Kessington, son of Sir Havan of Kessing, a wealthy territory not far from Salla City.

"Six months ago, Sir Havan was in a terrible hunting accident," she said. She could scarcely look at us while she told the story; instead, her eyes were fixed on her interlaced fingers. "Something frightened his horse, and the animal bolted. Sir Havan was thrown from the saddle, but his—his foot caught in the stirrup, and he was dragged along the ground..." When she resumed speaking her voice was even softer than before. "When they found him, his leg was broken, and his collar was broken and his neck—was broken—"

Samuel gave her one of the linen napkins. She pressed it to her eyes and it came away damp. She still did not look at us.

"They did not think he would live," she continued. "But he did. His leg healed and all the cuts and bruises healed—but something else had broken, something in his neck. He cannot feel anything anywhere in his body—or, at least, they do not think he can. He does not react when his body is touched. But he cannot speak and tell us what he feels and what he does not feel—"

"He can't speak?" Samuel asked her. "Can he hear you? Can he think and see?"

"His eyes are open, and sometimes he moves them to follow activity. He can grunt and make noises, but they cannot be understood. We can't ever be sure he understands us, but Bella believes he can."

"Bella?"

"His wife. My husband's mother. She tends him night and day, she dribbles food down his throat and cleans him—" Leonora shuddered delicately. I took that to mean that caring for the invalid was no easy task. "She is devoted to him," she whispered.

"Who is looking after the affairs of Kessing?" Samuel wanted to know. It was a fair question. Kessing was a good-sized territory and its lord was absolute law for several thousand souls.

"Lady Bella and my husband divide much of the work between them," Leonora said. Once she had finished the harrowing tale of Sir Havan's accident, Leonora felt capable of facing us again. She lifted her drowned blue eyes and fixed them on Samuel. I wondered what sort of effect their limpid sweetness would have on him. "But at Kessing, we maintain the fiction that Sir Havan still rules."

"How is that done?" I asked.

She looked at me. "Sir Havan has always held a public audience twice a month at which any vassal or tenant could air a grievance or sue for a favor," she said. "He still holds these open meetings—we carry him out and set him upon a chair, and people recite their petitions. Bella and Errol actually decide the cases, but if they make a ruling with which he disagrees, he grunts and moans and twists in his chair. So they call back the petitioner and revise their original judgment."

"So he is able to communicate," Sam said thoughtfully.

"In a way."

"And he is able to understand what goes on around him."

"He seems to be."

"And yet his condition has not improved for six months?"

"It has not improved, it has not deteriorated. It has not changed at all."

"And what do your *halani* say? I assume you have consulted one or two."

A smile touched her sad lips. "Dozens. They have fed him no end of potions and chanted hundreds of spells over his head. Nothing has availed. His body remains broken and his spirit remains trapped."

"And so you want me to kill him," I said evenly.

She looked at me quickly, her blue eyes utterly serious. "I have always loved Sir Havan," she said. "He is a good man and he has done many good things. But I cannot bear to see him suffer so much, day after day, dependent on another's hand to feed him and bathe him and tend him. You don't understand—you never knew him—he was so alive, so active, so sure of himself. To see him like this ... *I* would not want to live in such a way. I would not condemn anyone to such a life."

"And why should Aesara be the one to murder him?" Sam asked bluntly. "If you have dozens of *halani* already at your fortress—"

"It is a terrible thing to ask another human being to take a life," she said quietly. "And it is, as you say, murder. If one of the resident *halani* were to commit such an act, and be discovered, he or she would be put to death as well. I cannot ask them to do it."

"And Aesara? What if someone discovered *she* had poured the poison into the lord's drink?" Sam asked. "You've asked it of *her*."

"No one knows her at Kessing," Leonora replied quickly.

"One person has already recognized her," he pointed out.

"But Aesara could come in disguise. No one would ever know she had been the one to kill him."

I smiled at Sam again. He was such an innocent. All the years of intrigue that I had witnessed at Verallis would stand me in good stead now. "No, and no one would ever be certain if he had been murdered or if he had merely died at last," I told Sam. "That is the other reason the lady would like to hire my services."

Sam looked from me to Leonora and back at me. "I don't understand."

I kept my eyes on Leonora and my voice casual. "It has been eleven years, but surely you remember the scandal that attended King Raever's death?" I asked. "He had been unwell for a few days—everyone knew this, for there are no secrets at Verallis—and I had mixed him a batch of potions to restore him to good health. Shortly after taking one of them, one night, he died. Did I kill him? Was he much sicker than anyone had supposed? Did some prince or courtier, knowing I might be blamed, mix a deadly philtre and administer it in place of mine? No one was ever completely certain—which is why, Samuel, my friend, I sit here with you today in Salla City instead of drifting over the scattered lands of Sorretis as smoke and ashes, having been burned at the stake for treason."

There was a short silence. Leonora did not like to say baldly that she was sure I had killed my king, although clearly she believed it. Sam offered no comment at all.

"I'm interested in knowing," I said, "what the lord's wife and son think about this idea of yours."

The blue eyes were utterly guileless; she met my gaze openly. "It was Bella's idea," she said softly. "She is the one who recognized you here a few months back."

My eyes narrowed. That could very well be the truth. I had seen the traveling coach bowl through Salla City and recognized the heraldry on the door, for all of Raever's vassals were known to me, at least by reputation. I had not gone to the trouble of ducking behind a doorway as the horses slowed and passed. I had not expected to be identified.

"And your husband?" I asked.

"He is not convinced. But he has said to me in private that it would be a blessing for his father if he should die."

"And who rules Kessing when Sir Havan is gone?"

"Errol. And if Errol should die without heirs, his sister."

"And what does she think of this scheme to dispatch her father?"

"She has not been informed."

I picked up my glass of wine, which, like Leonora's, was almost untouched. Even Sam had only taken one or two swallows. I sipped the sweet, heavy liquid meditatively and thought it over. Well, clearly this angelically fair woman would profit if the murder were carried out, but as the case was presented, it was hard to tell if that was her motive. Giving all the participants the benefit of the doubt, it could be that they truly planned a mercy killing for which the corpse itself would thank me. For which all of Kessing would thank me, no doubt. I knew how uneasy subjects and vassals could become when their leader fell ill or grew uncertain. But to coolly and with calculated forethought kill a man…

"When is the next public audience?" I asked her.

She tried to smother her hopeful look. "A week from today, *halana*," she said. "Will you come?"

I nodded slowly. "I think so. I want to see Sir Havan for myself. At that point I will decide whether I will help you or not."

"And if you decide to help me?"

"I will give you a potion to give to your lord."

It was nearly full dark by the time Leonora left. Sam escorted her out; when he returned to my table, he was carrying a fresh bottle of wine. We had drunk very little of the sweet, fruity stuff he had brought for his visitor, but this was a dry red wine Sam usually chose for his serious drinking. He had finished two glasses before either of us said a word.

"Why don't you go ahead and ask me?" I said finally. I had elected to stay with the sweeter vintage, and I was sipping it much more slowly.

He poured himself another glass. "Why did you agree to go to Kessing and look this lord over?"

I was surprised into a laugh. "That's not the question," I said.

"It's the question I'm interested in the answer to."

I raised my own glass and inhaled the heavy, honeyed aroma. I said, "The real question is: Did you kill King Raever, or did you not?"

"That's not something I would ask you," Sam said quietly.

"I have always wanted to know," I said, "if you recognized my name when I arrived here five years ago."

"I recognized it."

"And so you must have known the scandal that followed me across Sorretis?"

"I had heard it."

"And yet you never wondered whether or not you harbored a murderer in your establishment?"

"I did not care," he said deliberately. I had erased pain from his wife's body, and so he did not care what I had done to others. He added, "Then."

I pounced on the word. "Then? And now?"

He raised his eyes and regarded me steadily. It was a familiar look; he often studied me this way. I was never sure what he hoped to learn. "I have always thought that you probably know how to kill a man."

I swallowed some of my wine. "I do."

"And that you have probably, in fact, killed one or two in your life."

I took another swallow. "I have."

"And it has seemed to me that whatever reasons you would have had for such actions would satisfy me. So I didn't worry about it."

That easily. I had won a man's trust merely by keeping silence for five years. I leaned back against the bench and closed my eyes. "When I was first named *halana* rex," I said, "I was known more for healing than for killing. For I had quite extraordinary abilities. Some *halani* are born healers—they need only to lay their fingers upon a man to cure his disease or to knit together the severed fibers of his bones. I had such skills, in those days. I radiated power—my hands seemed to glow at night when I watched them in the dark."

I had consumed more of the wine than I had thought, for my head was beginning to ache and behind my closed eyes I felt the bar rock gently around me. "Five summers after I joined Raever's court," I said, "there was an epidemic. A plague. It swept through the villages on the roads leading to Verallis—it rampaged through the royal household—it laid low guards and servants and noble ladies and faithful vassals and visiting dignitaries. No one was safe. No one was spared.

"Except me. So strong were my healing powers that I never succumbed to illness. Naturally, I ran through the castle, wherever the sickness took root, laying my hands upon the afflicted ones and exorcising the plague. I went to the guardhouses and the guesthouses and the nearby inns and villas, to find felled bodies writhing on the beds and on the floors. On each hot cheek I laid my cool hands, and the disease was routed. I rode like a madwoman through the night to the nearest villages, and stretched my arms out so that twenty people at a time could crowd around me and scratch at my flesh and be healed just by touching me. So exhausted was I, after three days of riding, that I collapsed in the square of one of these villages, unconscious and unmoving. And still they brought the ill and the helpless to my side, and still they reached out to touch me, and still they were cured."

I was silent for a long moment. I had not noticed Sam finishing his last glass of wine, but now I heard him pour another one. "Yet it is not healing for which I am remembered," I said finally. "But for killing."

"You never answered my question," he said.

I opened my eyes and looked at him. The wine or the memories or the dim lighting of the bar made him look softer and younger than usual. "What question was that?"

"Why did you agree to go to Kessing and see the lord? You have not raised a hand to help a soul since the night you gave peace to my Mari."

I closed my eyes again. "Because Leonora was wrong," I said. "I did know Sir Havan of Kessing. Eleven years ago, when I lived at Verallis."

I had expected the public audience at Kessing to be gruesome, and it was. Like most of the major fortress holdings of Sorretis, Kessing was built of a heavy gray stone that even on sunny days seemed to enclose a gloomy chill. Inside was a huge chamber where all the supplicants gathered twice a month to make their requests of their lord. Such public audiences were often loud and boisterous affairs; but at Kessing, where the petitioners spoke to a pitiful shell of a man, the mood was sober and deeply depressing.

Sam had casually offered to accompany me on the journey, and I had casually accepted, but inwardly I had been extremely grateful for his escort. I was doubly grateful for his presence now, a solid bulk in this sea of strangers. We stood at the back of the enormous room, gazing over perhaps two hundred bodies, staring toward the dais at the far end where Sir Havan of Kessing had been installed.

Everything Leonora had said of him was true. His head lolled back on his unsupportive neck; his arms and legs hung uselessly down. He had been tied to a large, cushioned chair so that he seemed, at least, to be sitting up and facing us. But his slack mouth and unfocused eyes gave little evidence that his mind was engaged.

Beside him, Lady Bella knelt on an embroidered stool. Leonora stood behind him, gazing down at the inexpressive face. Sir Errol stood at the head of the stage, a herald beside him to call out names, and gravely listened to each petition. It was not a cheery or inspiring scene.

"What do you think of the lord's wife?" I whispered in Sam's ear, as we watched the slow procession.

"She seems to genuinely love the man," he whispered back. "It's a hard thing to counterfeit under such conditions."

I nodded. "And his son?"

"He seems capable enough, but not a happy man."

"Does he want his father dead?"

"Wouldn't you," Sam said slowly, "if your father lived like this?"

"And the son's wife?"

Only once had Leonora lifted her head and surveyed the crowd. Within minutes, she had spotted us. I could see the color of her eyes even across the wide stone floor. She had not smiled or nodded, but merely dropped her gaze again to her father-in-law's face.

"She's ambitious, I think," Sam said slowly. "But she does not look cruel."

"Tell me," I said. "What would you choose, if you were Sir Havan of Kessing? Would you want to continue to live, imprisoned in such a wreck of a body? Or would you want some kind soul to mete out the poison that would let you die, quietly and in peace?"

"I would drink the poison, and gladly," Sam said.

"So would I."

For a few moments longer, I watched Sir Havan across the room. As I had told Sam, I had known Havan and Lady Bella, but not well, and that had been eleven years ago. He had been a laughing, virile, confrontational man who had had as many friends as enemies at Verallis. Raever had trusted him, though they had disagreed often enough, and spectacularly enough, to be considered wary allies. I had not dealt much with court politics, but of course I had met most of the personalities of the day, and Havan had been one of the brightest.

He had not been at Verallis when Raever died. He had not been one of those who accused me or defended me. I wondered what opinion he had, in fact, held of me—not that the knowledge would influence me one way or the other now.

We had been there maybe an hour when a strange commotion erupted on the dais. Sir Errol had just pronounced some sentence on a cowed-looking farmer, when the mangled body of Sir Havan made a violent reaction. Even from this distance, we could hear the formless grunts and whines. We could see the head shake and the shoulders twitch against the sides of the chair. Leonora's hands flew to her cheeks. Bella's fingers wrapped themselves around her husband's wrist. Errol crossed to his father's side and bent over the shivering body as if to try and understand the indecipherable sounds. He turned back to the man he had just dismissed.

"Wait!" he called out. "My father has reversed the judgment."

On the words, Sir Havan grew calm again. The dejected man straightened and made a field-hand's salute toward the stage. "My lord," he said, and backed into the crowd. All around us the audience murmured in a muffled unease.

"I can't stand this," I said. I found that my fingers had clutched Samuel's arm in a grip that must have been painful; I dropped my hand.

"Do you want to leave?" he asked.

I shook my head. "I owe Havan the courtesy of staying long enough to be certain."

And so we stayed, through each grim petition, each inaudible argument. Havan did not again attempt to communicate. It was with indescribable relief that I saw the last petitioner make his case, hear his judgment, bow, and rejoin the assembly. Now what? Everyone appeared to be waiting for some cue, some gesture of release. I saw activity on the dais and realized that four footmen had lifted the lord's chair and now were carrying it carefully off the stage, down through the ranks of petitioners, and toward the exit. No one would leave the room before the lord. As the crowd divided, Sam and I found ourselves along the aisle that opened between the dais and the door. Wordlessly, we watched as Havan was carried toward us, his arms flopping against the sides of the chair, his gaze running wildly around the circle of watching faces.

He saw me and his eyes locked on mine.

It was as if he tried to lunge from the chair. His body spasmed and one of his feet kicked out, landing with considerable force against a footman's chin. The servant stumbled, lost his grip, and came to his knees, desperately trying to keep his hold. Bella screamed from the stage. The crowd loosed a collective gasp of dismay and stepped backward as if to avoid contamination.

The other footmen hastily settled the chair on the floor as Sam strode over to offer assistance. I trailed reluctantly behind. "Shall I call for help?" Sam asked. "Do you want me to carry one leg?"

"No, no, I just lost my balance," said the shaken servant.

I paid little attention to the conference between Sam and the footmen; I ignored the sound of Bella's footsteps hurrying across the hall. Havan was still staring at me, still trembling in his seat. His mouth worked as if he would speak the most urgent message. He recognized me, that was clear. He knew what I was capable of. Did he want to shriek at me to go away, to leave him alone, to take my sorcerous potions elsewhere?

Did he want to beg me to release him?

I knelt before him and took one nerveless hand in mine, feeling the fingers lax and chilly. As soon as I touched him, he grew still; he stopped his frantic jerking. Even his eyes seemed more serene, though they never wavered from my face. I could read that look, I thought. *Do what you can for me.* I squeezed his fingers, then dropped his hand as Bella came skidding to a halt beside him. I did not want her to see me again, to guess why I had come. I stepped back into the silent crowd and turned my face away until Havan had finally been carried out the door.

We had agreed to meet Leonora at a small inn just outside the fortress gates. She came to us that evening with another cadre of guards in the blue-and-gold livery of Kessing.

"Well?" she asked the instant she was shown into our room. "Do you believe now that I told you the truth?"

"I believe you," I said wearily. I had mixed up a potion as soon as we entered the inn. I had sworn to never again interfere in the lives of others, but it is easier to break a promise to yourself than to break a promise to someone else. "No one should have to live like that."

I handed her the vial, wrapped in blue silk, the color of her eyes. She took it from me with those eyes at their widest. "This is it? Already? This is the potion?" she asked, almost stammering. "What must be done?"

"He must drink all of it," I said. "There is not much and it has no flavor. It can be mixed in wine or water. He will not know what he is taking."

She unwrapped the vial and stared at the clear liquid through the glass. "And it will not hurt him?" she whispered. "He will feel no pain?"

"None, I swear to you," I said.

Quickly she rewrapped the philtre and tucked it inside her reticule. I wondered exactly how she planned to administer this to him, but decided not to ask. She seemed quite resourceful. "What do I owe you?" she wanted to know.

I shook my head. "I want nothing from you."

"But—surely—I have brought gold with me, and jewels—"

"This is not a service for which I wish to be paid," I said quietly.

She hesitated a moment, then nodded. "Very well," she said. "On behalf of Sir Havan and his family, I thank you."

"I don't want thanks, either," I said.

She could see that I would not take her hand, but she required something more of a leavetaking, so she offered her hand to Sam. He took it gravely, shook it, and released her. "Goodbye, my lady," he said, and ushered her toward the door.

I was staring out the single small window, but I knew he had turned back to watch me once he locked Leonora out. "Do you want to leave for Salla City first thing in the morning?" he asked.

It was not quite dusk, and the trek would take us several hours. "No," I said, "I want to leave tonight. Now."

We did not push the horses, and in fact the cool, starlit journey was almost pleasant. In the night air, sounds seemed to be invested with a strange significance; each hoofbeat, each jingle of the bridle sounded distinct and mysterious in the plush silence. We encountered no other travelers on the way.

We had been riding for nearly two hours when I began, without prompting, to tell my story. "Raever was dying," I said. "I was the only one who knew it. He had contracted a disease of the blood for which I did not have the remedy. I tried—Leith and Egeva, how I tried—to produce an antidote that would save him, but there are some diseases, I have learned, for which there are no cures. He was not in great pain—that much, as you know, I could do for him—but his body was growing frail and his memory had become unreliable. As I said, no one but me knew just how sick he was, and me he had sworn to secrecy.

"Raever did not fear many things, but he had an absolute abhorrence of weakness, of dependency. He hated to see someone beg—he did not even care much for humility. The idea of a gradual, wasting illness, which would leave him utterly at the mercy of others, was terrible to him. And so he asked me for a philtre that would release him early into death."

I fell silent a moment. Samuel made no comment. Had I not seen his fingers shift upon the reins, I would have thought he was asleep. "At first, I refused, for he was my king and I did not want him to die. Also, I had not yet despaired of finding a cure. But no more than he could, could I bear to see him fall into faintness and delirium, and we agreed that if he were to die by his own hand, it should be while he was still able to rationally choose such a death.

"It was Raever who came up with the plan. He had me mix up a month's supply of potions, all in separate, identical bottles. Twenty-nine of them would be filled with a few harmless ounces of water—only one would carry the death dosage inside. He would drink one every night before he went to bed, destroying the bottle before he slept so that no one would find it and later suspect that I had given him poison. He chose this method," I added, "because he said that no man, even one who wanted to die, should know with certainty the hour of his death."

"And did you in fact present him with the thirty bottles?" Samuel asked at last.

"I did."

"And upon which night did he die?"

I whispered, "The twenty-third."

"It seems to me," Sam said, his voice slow and comforting in the dark, "that a king as clever as Raever was said to be would know that suspicion would fall on you, no matter how careful he was with these bottles."

"Oh, he knew it. I knew it. He wanted me to leave Verallis a few days before he began taking his nightly potions, so I would not be there for any inquisition. But I could not bear to leave him while he was still alive, while there still might be something I could do for him, however small. I was prepared for the maelstrom that followed. At that, I did not greatly care if they condemned me to death or allowed me to live. Not much really mattered to me once Raever was dead."

"You loved him," Sam said.

"He had a wife and three daughters, and he was twenty years older than I was."

"Yet you loved him," Sam repeated stubbornly.

"I *believed* in him," I said. "He was an autocratic and domineering man, but he had such vision and strength of purpose. There was nothing he could have asked me to do that I would not have done, for it seemed to me that this man, more clearly than anyone I had ever met, understood right and wrong in the largest sense. I am not the only one from whom he commanded great devotion. We were a court of disciples, and we fell apart when our leader died."

"And yet I hear good things about his daughter, who is now the queen."

"Yes," I said wearily. "She is an intelligent woman and she rules well. But she is not Raever. Something went out of the world when Raever died."

"Something went out of you," he said.

I looked over at him, but I could not see much in the dark. "What do you mean?"

"You're the healer," he said. "Mend your own broken heart."

"*Your* heart has been broken," I said swiftly. "Do you think it is an easy thing to fix?"

"I think," he replied carefully, "that someone with the right skills could heal me."

I faced forward again. The road ahead looked endless. "There are some things for which there are no cures," I said.

It might have been my imagination, but I thought I heard him sigh. We rode on into the unchanging darkness.

Naturally, I slept late the next day. It had only been a few hours before dawn when Sam and I arrived in Salla City. He had accompanied me to the cottage I had rented on the edge of town, watched me dismount, and taken the reins of my horse. It was, after all, his horse. He did not say good-bye as he rode away, and I did not look back at him as I let myself into my unlit house.

Now it was late afternoon, and I was, surprisingly, hungry. I had not eaten for nearly twenty-four hours, but still, hunger was a sensation I rarely experienced. I rose and moved aimlessly about my cottage, but there was very little in the cupboards which could be turned into a meal. I felt a curious reluctance to go to Sam's for dinner, certain as I was that he would join me for the meal. I knew better than to rely on the gentleness and seeming strength of any man. I had gone so long without yielding my burdens to anyone. What made me long now to take my comfort from somebody else's heart?

I shook my head and concentrated on putting together a makeshift meal from some moldy biscuits and a vinegary jug of wine. Out of habit, I pulled out my zafo cards and shuffled them. Mostly to distract myself, I laid out a standard grid and turned the cards over in my own unconventional order.

The primary significator: the hooded figure. The final outcome: the black queen. I smiled faintly. These same two cards had appeared in the last reading I had done, only then their positions had been reversed. Now the shadowy, unformed image was in my past, and in my future was the assured, powerful, dark-haired woman. What had I left behind, then, and what was I to become?

The four cards in the second row, the pictures of my past, showed more hazy and undefined images. There, the secretive moon that refused to answer questions; there, the locked box, showing that treasures had been denied. Again, the black king reversed. Beside him, the roan stallion, who bespoke restlessness, travel and change.

In the third row, all was altered. A stack of twelve coins indicated the richness of my fortune, and a blazing sun shone upon my home. The white king appeared to answer the questions of my heart, and in the position that indicated career, the winged horse spread its alabaster wings. This last card was the elemental symbol for air and had been taken by the *halani* to mean magical ability. A rebirth of my power; a professional renaissance.

I chewed on another stale biscuit and thought for a moment. Clearly, it was going to be impossible to keep the events of Kessing a secret. I had known that before I undertook the journey. Bella had recognized me on the street and had spoken my name at least once. She would be even more likely to mention it again after all this. If I stayed in Salla City, I would be found. If I was found, there were others who would bring requests to me of a dangerous and highly emotional nature. I had sworn never to interfere again in the lives of others, but Raever had made me take another vow.

"Promise me you will not kill yourself after I am dead," he had said. I had been amazed. How had he known about the second vial I had mixed up, giving one to him and keeping one for myself? "Promise me this disease will only take one life."

And because I had been unable to refuse him anything, I had promised, but I had only in the most rudimentary way kept my vow. You could not say I had really lived in the past eleven years.

Except for the last couple of days, when once again I had held life and death in my hands, and shuddered at the responsibility.

I picked up the white king and studied it a moment. A fair-haired man, or a good man, or an old man; the card meant all of these things. I had not looked for such a card in such a position at such a time in my life.

Outside, I heard the gate squeal on the unoiled hinges, and running footsteps crossed the gravel walk. I did not have much time to debate whether or not I would answer the door before it was flung open and Sam strode into the room. He had never before entered my house, for he had never been invited in, and I stared at him in astonishment.

He was laughing. Before I could move toward him or away, he was upon me. He grabbed me around the waist and lifted me in the air. I clutched at his shoulders to keep my balance, staring down at him in excitement and alarm.

"Samuel Berris!" I cried out. "What are you doing?"

He actually tossed me once in the air once before setting me on my feet. Then he hugged me and finally let me go.

"The news from Kessing arrived this morning," he said.

I made a big show of smoothing my hair down after the unexpected rough treatment. "It did?" I said coldly.

"It was a miracle, they say. None of the *halani* can explain it. Sir Havan of Kessing awoke this morning a whole man, with all his limbs answering the call of his will and his mind completely sharp. He is weak, of course, and they think it will be some time before he walks again under his own power, but he is well, he is healed. There has been a general rejoicing throughout Kessing."

"I'm sure there has been," I said. "Who brought the news to Salla City?"

"Some peddler. Not the Lady Leonora."

"I wonder how she reacted to the news this morning," I said.

Sam grinned. "She is a most dutiful and loving daughter-in-law," he said. "I'm sure she fell to her knees in gratitude."

"I doubt she will ever thank me personally," I said.

Sam was watching me, some of his elation tempered now with speculation. "Lady Bella will, though," he said. "Or the lord himself. You cannot expect this secret to be kept."

"No," I said. "I can't."

"And will you be here when they come?" he asked. "And when the others come, with terrible stories of dying lords and sick children and beloved mothers wracked with pain? Will you be here when travelers come to Salla City, looking for you?"

I glanced around the rented cottage. Perhaps I could have done more with it, changed the curtains or stocked the larder. "I don't care much for this place," I said. "That's why I spent so much time in your tavern."

"I have a house that is too big for one," he said. "And it's very close to the tavern."

I looked at him. "I thought your heart was broken," I said.

"I know a healer," he replied.

"I will be traveling a lot," I said. "None of these sick mothers and crying babies will be able to journey to Salla City."

"I like to travel," he said. "Groyce can mind the bar."

"Then I suppose I will stay in Salla City," I said.

"Good," he said, "I'll help you pack."

Not that there was much to transfer to the small, welcoming house behind the tavern. Groyce and Sam carried the heavier items I elected to keep. Lina helped me organize my clothes. She smiled at me shyly, and for the first time in the five years that I had known her, I attempted to make conversation.

"I'm glad you're staying," she told me when I asked her how she was. "I'm going to have a baby."

It was not quite dark yet, and we had just moved the last of my things into Sam's house, when one of the girls from the tavern ran over with more news. A delegation had been spotted on the road, led by a virtual army of blue-and-gold-clad guards.

"So soon?" I murmured, wiping dust from my face.

"They're late," Sam said. "They should have been here by noon."

"Who are they?" Groyce asked. "Friends of the noble-woman who was here?"

"Friends of Aesara's," Sam said. He took my hand, and we went outside together to greet the travelers.

# Wintermoon Wish

All the way from Wodenderry to Merendon, I sat alone in the coach and scowled. I couldn't believe that no one, not even my cousin Renner, was willing to leave the royal city and miss the queen's ball.

But I had never spent a Wintermoon away from my grandparents' inn in Merendon, and I was not about to start now. Now that the whole world was bleak and my life nothing but a blighted promise.

My aunt tells me I am a fanciful girl with a flair for the dramatic. My mother says more plainly that I overreact to everything. In this instance, at any rate, I was sure I had a broken heart and nothing would mend it except a trip to Merendon, and even that didn't seem likely to do the trick. But who would want to stay in Wodenderry, when Trevor was in love with Corrinne and taking her to the Wintermoon ball?

The weather was bitterly cold and even my father's well-built carriage could not keep out the drafts. Even our frequent stops for hot tea at little inns along the way were not enough to warm me all the way through. By the time we arrived in Merendon, just around sunset, my feet were icicles in their fashionable fur-lined boots and I couldn't feel my fingers in my gloves. We pulled up in front of the Leaf & Berry Inn and my heart sank. There were no welcome lights pouring from the front door or the upper-story windows. The inn looked as dark and cold as the interior of the coach.

But when the driver carried my luggage around back to the kitchen door, my spirits rose again. I could see my grandmother through the window, working at the stove, her white hair piled on top of her head, her hands busy, her face serene. I could smell the baking bread and roasting chicken. The very shape and scent of the scene before me matched the picture of *home* I always carried in my heart.

I was almost in tears as I burst through the door, and my grandmother dropped her spoon with a clatter. "Lirril! You startled me. Oh, look at you, you're half-frozen. Come sit by the stove. Bob! Build up a fire in the parlor! Lirril's here and she's a little ice-child."

I felt better than I had for days.

My grandfather bustled in, gathered me in a big hug, paid a handsome tip to the driver, and made sure the man had a place to spend the night. I sat at the kitchen table, sipping tea and inhaling the smells of the house. Dinner and wine and pie in here; wax and polish and soap drifting in from the other rooms. Overlaying it all, a sharper, sweeter odor, the very scent of Wintermoon.

"You've started the wreath already, haven't you?" I said, my voice just a touch accusatory. "You knew I was coming, and you couldn't wait until I got here?"

My grandmother merely smiled. "We've gathered some spruce and some rowan, and I've put some greens over the banister, but we haven't finished braiding the wreath," she said. "Don't worry, you'll have plenty to do."

"A mighty cold Wintermoon it's going to be," my grandfather observed, stepping out the door to fetch another pile of wood. "Glad you made it here before the snow. Supposed to start falling tomorrow afternoon."

In a few moments, the three of us were gathered cozily around the kitchen table, eating my grandmother's excellent meal and catching up on events. Well, mostly *I* told *them* everything that had been happening to me lately. Their lives tended not to hold much excitement or variation, so what did they have to tell? *Oh, we had three guests come through last week, and a family of five stopped here the week before. Things were slow over the summer, but that gave us time to sew new curtains and finish the floors in the back bedroom on the second floor.* I had far more to relate.

I hadn't planned to bring up Trevor's name, but my grandmother had an uncannily good memory, which sometimes came in handy and sometimes did not. "What about that boy?" she asked as she served the pie. "The one you were so keen on this summer? Trevor? Was that his name?"

"Oh, I'm not interested in him anymore," I said, my voice quite airy. "He's—well, he's—anyway, Corrinne has been flirting with him most shamelessly. So of course he's practically infatuated with her. He even wrote her a poem a couple of weeks ago. A poem! Did you ever hear of such a silly thing?"

I had been shockingly jealous when Corrinne showed it to us—to me, and the other girls from my school who had formed a circle of friends. It wasn't a very good poem, it didn't even rhyme, but you could tell by its extravagant praise how much Trevor adored her. I had been in love with Trevor all my life—or, at least, since he had danced with me two years ago when I was fourteen and allowed to go to my first Summermoon ball at the palace. But he had never so much as written my name on a calling card to be left at my parents' house.

My grandparents looked amused. "Never was much of one for poems myself," my grandfather said. "Still, that seems like a powerful sign of attraction. Man who'd write a poem for a girl would do anything for her, I suppose."

"I wonder if your father ever wrote a poem for your mother," my grandmother said to me.

"He would have if she'd asked him to," my grandfather spoke up. "That man would have done anything she wanted. He courted her for months. He's still courting her, all these years later."

Revolted, I put up my hands. "Please. Stop."

"I'm going to ask him about that poem," my grandfather said, teasing me.

My grandmother stood. "I'm going to clear the dishes. You two get started on the wreath."

The best part of Wintermoon: braiding the wreath. I happily settled on the floor beside my grandfather and helped him plait the long, whippy branches together, tying them at intervals with red and gold cords. My fingers were soon sticky with sap and I had sharp little needles all over my dress. My grandmother joined us about thirty minutes later, carrying a basket of odds and ends.

"Oh, here's a few pearls from that necklace that broke … let's tie those on. Those will be for—well, what do you think? A wedding? Yes, pearls for a wedding. And some of that blue silk from the back bedroom. How about serenity? Now don't forget the dried fruit—that's for prosperity, Lirril, never make a wreath without it."

My grandfather had his own contributions—dried cedar chips and a bird's wing and a scrap of fabric from a ship's ripped sail—though sometimes his connections between object and the magic they could confer seemed tenuous at best. I had only one extra bit to bind into the wreath, a long ribbon embroidered with alternating hearts and birds.

"That's for love," I said, knotting it around the woven branches.

"That's something everyone needs every year," my grandmother said.

When we were done, my grandfather hung the great wreath over the fireplace and it made a dense shape of promise over the mantel. Tomorrow night we would build a bonfire in the back, between the chatterleaf and kirren-berry trees that gave the inn its name, and we would throw the wreath into the blaze. All our hopes for the new year written in flame. Guaranteed to come true.

I slept deeply and well—for the first time in days—in the small bedroom on the third floor. It was the room that had belonged to my mother and her twin when they were growing up. Even once I woke, I didn't realize how far advanced the morning was, because so little light was coming in the double windows. When I finally rose and dressed and peeked outside, I understood why: Snow was falling so heavily that the sky was leaden and gray. The clouds were piled so deeply overhead that I couldn't imagine the sun would ever shine.

I skipped downstairs, calling, "Look at the snow! Look at it! There must be two feet on the ground already!" I didn't care much for snow on the crowded streets of Wodenderry, but here in Merendon, where I didn't need to leave the inn for a single necessity, snow was a delight.

"No one will be traveling far this day," my grandmother observed. "So anyone who has somewhere to get on Wintermoon had better be there by now."

I danced around the kitchen. "No one's here—we've got the inn all to ourselves," I exclaimed. "We can eat all the pie—and drink all the cider—and stay up as late as we want. No guests! No chores!"

My grandmother laughed. My grandfather said, "I'll just go chop some more wood."

Half an hour later, the stage from Oakton arrived.

It came feeling its way through the blizzard like a blind child down a stairwell and arrived at the front door like an omen of doom. My grandfather ran out to exchange a few words with the coachman. I watched as the door to the coach pushed open—a maneuver that took some effort against the wind—and a single figure stepped out, landing knee-deep in the drift of snow. He was tall and reedy, wearing an inadequate coat against the searing chill of the weather, and his head was uncovered. I could see his face, angular and thin, and his eyes, dark and devoid of hope. He couldn't have been more than a year or two older than I was, but he looked weighed down by cares or disappointments. A more pitiful, dispirited, unwelcome visitor you could not imagine having arrive on your doorstep on Wintermoon.

"Oh, no," I breathed as he fought his way up the walk toward the front door. "Oh, *no*."

My grandmother had materialized beside me and was looking out the front door, serene as always. She said, "Looks like we've got company for Wintermoon."

His name was Jake. That was about all we learned about him during dinner that night, and I wasn't even interested in that much information. The four of us sat around the bigger table in the dining room and passed around food while we made labored conversation. His name was Jake, he was headed toward Thrush Hollow. He was sorry to be caught in the storm, yes, ma'am, so glad there was a place that could take him in, he was sorry if he was any trouble. He had the money to pay. He was polite and, once he'd warmed up a little, not unattractive in an intense and moping fashion. But who wanted strangers around on Wintermoon? Wintermoon was a time for family! For being with the people you loved most in the world! There was almost never anyone in the inn on Wintermoon. Why hadn't he started his journey a day or two earlier if he was so eager to join up with his parents or siblings or cousins or whomever he was off to visit? Why was he *here, now,* with *my* family, spoiling *my* Wintermoon? I could not have been unhappier if I had still been in Wodenderry.

Well, yes, I could have. But not much.

"So, Jake, would you like to help me build the bonfire?" my grandfather asked in his genial way as we finished the pie. I must admit, even though we'd had to share it, there was plenty of pie for everyone. "It's dark enough now."

Jake came to his feet, looking uncertain. "You build a bonfire? Do you burn a wreath, too?"

"Well, goodness, doesn't everybody?" my grandmother exclaimed.

Jake gave her a crooked grin and looked, for the first time, boyish. "I haven't. Not for years."

"You don't have to help," my grandfather said.

"He wants to," my grandmother replied briskly. "Go on out there, you two. Lirril and I will clear the dishes. We'll come out when the fire's good and hot."

Jake put on his threadbare coat and followed my grandfather out the kitchen door to where most of the fire had already been laid. I watched from the window as they brushed away the accumulated snow and searched for dry kindling. Jake moved slowly, like a man at an unfamiliar task, but willingly, as if learning something he would like to know. Twice I saw him smile at something my grandfather said. He had only smiled once throughout the entire meal.

"He seems like a nice boy," my grandmother said, scrubbing at the dishes.

I sniffed. "How can you tell? He hardly said a word."

"Looks like he's had a hard life, though."

"He's so wretched he's pathetic."

My grandmother gave me one of her rare looks of disapproval. Her eyes were an odd blue, pale but pretty; my own eyes were exactly the same color. "Better to be pathetic than to be cruel," she said

My eyes widened. "I wasn't mean to him!"

"See that you aren't," she said.

I had just wiped down the table when Jake came back inside. "Bob says I should get the wreath down," he said in an apologetic voice, as if he thought it was something that would upset us. My grandmother just nodded, but I was instantly antagonized.

"It's not *time* to burn the wreath yet," I said. "We *never* burn it 'til midnight."

Jake nodded somberly. "No. That's what he said. He thought maybe I'd have something to bind to the branches."

I was frowning, but my grandmother was nodding. "That's a good idea. What would you like to add in?"

Jake looked despondent. "I don't know. Nothing I can think of."

"Nonsense. Everyone has a wish at Wintermoon," my grandmother said. "Come help me take it down, and Lirril and I will tell you all the wishes we've tied onto it so far. Then you can tell us what it's missing."

We put this plan into action, although—as I could have foretold—none of our blue silk and bird feathers and cedar chips inspired Jake to articulate his own desires. He did finger my embroidered ribbon and look wistful when my grandmother told him it represented love.

"Man-and-woman love or home-and-family love?" he asked.

"Either. Both," my grandmother said firmly.

"And these dried apricots—these mean a happy home?"

"A prosperous one," my grandmother corrected. "But, now, I like that. Let's find something to stand for a warm house, filled with joy. Jake, what did you bring that we can tie to the wreath?"

His expression was a little bitter. "Nothing you can use for that, I'm afraid."

"No, I'll pull a splinter from the front sign and tie that on with some ribbon. No place happier than the Leaf & Berry! Though that sign is a disgrace. More than twenty years old now, so weathered you almost can't read the lettering. There's paint in the barn, but Bob hasn't had a minute to sit down and put on a fresh coat." She paused, remembered why she had started her sentence, and continued. "But that's not what I meant. We need something of yours to wrap around the wreath. So you're part of the celebration. So your own wishes will catch on fire. Then, you know, they're more likely to come true."

Smiling a little, Jake investigated his pockets to reveal them almost empty. It didn't take much imagination to picture his single duffel bag to be almost as bare. I couldn't imagine that he would have a thing worth contributing to our bonfire, but I knew my grandmother well enough to know she would not be satisfied until we had *something* of Jake's to throw in the flames tonight.

"What about the top button on your shirt?" I asked. "It's about to fall off, anyway." My grandmother gave me a look that I couldn't interpret, so I added, "Or I could get a needle and thread and sew it back on for you."

Jake lifted a hand and yanked the button off with one quick pull. "No, I'll be happy to donate it to the wreath," he said. "It's metal, though—I don't know if it will burn."

"Then you can rescue it tomorrow morning and sew it back on," my grandmother said. "Something that survives the fire is always luck."

Soon enough we had attached our last contributions and leaned the wreath against the wall. My grandfather came stamping in, alternately rubbing his ears and blowing on his fingers. "*Mighty* cold out," he observed. "Believe I'll come in for a spell and warm up. Lirril, do you and Jake want to go out and watch the fire for a while?"

Jake looked surprised at the invitation, but I was already on my feet; I'd known it was coming. That was the tradition at the Leaf & Berry. My grandfather always started the fire, then he let someone else tend it 'til midnight, when the wreath was thrown on. Then he and my grandmother stayed up 'til dawn, watching the flames, shooing everyone else back inside so they could be alone before the dying fire. I had always wondered what made Wintermoon such a special holiday for the two of them. Neither my mother nor my aunt knew the answer.

"Go on. You two young ones keep the fire going," my grandmother said, waving us toward the door. "We'll come out later."

So I pulled on my gloves and my winter coat and my fur-lined boots and followed Jake out the kitchen door. The snow had stopped falling but lay thick on the ground like acres of profligate diamonds. The bonfire was a brilliant living jewel against the sere dark. The air was so cold that for a minute I lost the ability to breathe. I ran through the snowdrifts to hover as close to the fire as I could bear. Jake followed more slowly but came just as close. For a while we stood in silence, stretching our hands out to the flames, inhaling the scents of cedar and spruce and snow.

It occurred to me that Jake was not the most talkative of people, and that the night was going to be extremely dull and extremely long if we passed it in silence, and that if I wanted conversation, I was going to have to initiate it myself. I glared resentfully into the dark, and then sighed and glanced over at him.

"So, Jake," I said. "I take it your family lives in Thrush Hollow?"

He eyed me uncertainly. "Some of them. An uncle and some cousins."

"Do you always spend Wintermoon with them?"

"No."

I waited, but he had no more to add. "Where do you come from? Did you ride the stage all the way from Oakton?"

He nodded.

I found myself starting to wish I was keeping the Wintermoon vigil by myself. "What do you do there? I'm guessing you have a job?"

He nodded again. "Had one. Worked in a carpenter's shop. I did a lot of the staining and painting. I wasn't that good with the lathe and tools."

I could hardly miss his use of the past tense. "But you don't work there now?"

"Now I'm moving to Thrush Hollow."

"To be with your uncle?" That elicited another nod. "That'll be nice." He shrugged.

I let the silence run out for a good long while. Long enough for the flames to die down and for Jake to carefully pile on a few more logs. Long enough for him to glance at me, glance away, look back at the house, cut his eyes in my direction again. I was feeling anything but kindly, but I gave him a nod meant to be encouraging. *Go ahead. Your turn to ask questions.*

"Um," he said. "So they call you Lirril?" I nodded. He said, "I never came across that name before."

"It's a mirror name," I said. He looked blank. "It's the same forward and backward. My grandmother's and grandfather's names, too. Hannah and Bob. It's something our family does."

"And you live here with your grandparents?"

"No. I live in Wodenderry with my mother and father. But we always come to Merendon for Wintermoon and I didn't want to miss it this year just because—" I shut my mouth with a snap.

"Because?"

I shrugged. "Oh, there's a ball there, and everyone wanted to attend, but *I* didn't want to go, I wanted to be *here*, and so I came to the inn while they stayed behind. They'll be here tomorrow, though, with my aunt and my uncle and my cousin Renner." I shot a look up at the sky. "If it's stopped snowing. If the roads are clear."

"Why didn't you want to go to the ball?" he asked.

Why would he think to ask that? And his voice was so soft, so serious, as if he really cared to know the answer. I shrugged again, not quite so pettishly. "Because my feelings were hurt. Because I was afraid it would make me sad. There's a man I know and he—" I hunched my shoulders. "And I'd rather be here. I love it here."

"I would, too," he agreed. "If I had a place like this to go to? I wouldn't wait 'til Wintermoon. I'd stay here all the time."

I was starting to think I could guess the answer for myself, and I didn't even want to *know* it, but I asked anyway. "So where are your parents?"

"Dead," he said flatly.

He added nothing to the single word. "I'm—that's—I'm sorry," I stammered. "When did—what happened?"

Now he was the one to give a shrug. "My mother died a long time ago. My father last year."

I could scarcely imagine such a thing. "What did you do without them?"

A ghost of a smile. "Worked. Found a place to stay. I did all right."

"But what about your family? Your aunts and uncles and grandparents? Why didn't you go to them?"

"I'm going now. To my uncle."

I had a sudden dreadful premonition. "Does he know you're coming?"

Jake almost laughed. "No."

"Will he be happy to see you?"

Jake looked lost for a moment, young. My age or even younger. "I don't know. He and my father hadn't spoken for years. He doesn't even know my father's dead. I just thought—it was worth a try. I don't have anywhere else to go."

"Why couldn't you stay in Oakton?"

"I could. I'll go back, I guess, if things don't work out in Thrush Hollow. But the carpenter I worked for sold his shop and the new owner had sons of his own to do the work and I—there wasn't a place for me there. I was always curious about my uncle. Seemed like as good a time as any to find out what he was like."

I felt so sorry for him that I almost despised him. Who could be so wretched and alone? Who could be so adrift in the world? I didn't want to wonder what his life might be like, so different from my own. I closed my heart and glanced away.

"I'm sure you'll like Thrush Hollow," I said, my voice indifferent. "Everyone says it's very pretty."

He caught my tone, rebuffed as I meant him to be. He merely nodded and did not answer. He watched the fire a little longer, then added a couple more logs. The old ones collapsed in a shower of sparks, which flung themselves into the snow and hissed out. Neither of us so much as winced away.

Now a determined silence held us both. I could feel my feet turning to ice inside my plush boots, and my cheeks ached with cold. Overhead, the sky was impossibly clear; the hard stars looked merciless. The full moon was so white and so brilliant it could have been sculpted from fresh snow. I wondered how much longer we had 'til midnight.

Jake added more fuel to the fire, then stood a moment with his back to the flames, as if to warm the other half of his body. I noted crossly that his coat was too thin. He must be even colder than I was.

"You should be wearing something heavier than that," I said.

He just looked at me for a moment. "This will do," he said.

I shrugged. Fine. If he didn't want to go in and put on a sweater, I didn't care.

We were quiet for another long stretch. The fire shifted again and the flames contracted, licking their small orange tongues around the charred embers of the bottom logs. Jake knelt to poke at the templed branches, teasing the fire back out. I accidentally glanced down at the bottoms of his feet.

"You have *holes* in your *shoes!*" I exclaimed. "What are you—you could get *frostbite* out here on a night like this!"

He gave me a dark look but didn't answer, merely continued prodding at the fire 'til the blaze caught again. He knelt there a while longer to make sure the fire was really going, then he stood up. "I'm fine," he said. "I rarely feel the cold."

I stared at him. "*Everybody* feels the cold on a night like this! Why don't you—I'll watch the fire. You go put on another pair of shoes."

"This is the only pair I have," he said quietly.

I stared at him a moment, hating him more than I had ever hated anyone in my life. "Very well," I said through gritted teeth. "You watch the fire." And I stomped back into the house, so angry that I almost slammed the door behind me, so furious that I was almost blinded by the emotion. Or blinded by something. I bumped into the kitchen door and stumbled a little as I turned into the hallway. I wasn't crying, though. No, I certainly wasn't. I brought a candle with me and set it on the hall table, then peered into the closet and began to root around.

Ten minutes later I was back outside, and I practically flung a few items to the ground at Jake's feet. "Here. Put that on. It's my father's coat." No surprise that Jake didn't answer. I continued in a hard, fast voice. "He never wears it unless he's here and the weather's so cold he can't endure it. He says it's the most unfashionable cut imaginable and no man with any taste would ever wear it." I nudged the other pieces over with my toe. "Same thing about the boots. He won't put them on. He keeps trying to give them away, but no one will take them. They're ugly, but they're warm. I brought you some socks, too."

Jake didn't make a move. "I can't take those things."

"Well, you can wear them for a night, can't you? No one else needs them this very minute. It's stupid not to put them on and then freeze to death because you were proud and stubborn."

His eyes dropped; he looked longingly at the warm wool coat. "I could pay you something," he said.

"No, you couldn't! You could just be reasonable and put this coat on. *And* these boots. Here. Give me your coat. Give it to me right now."

And I stepped up to him and started unbuttoning his own garment, tattered and miserable as it was. Two of the buttons came off in my hands; something else to tie to the wreath if we had a little time and some extra ribbon. He resisted a moment, his face creased with doubt, but I started yanking at the sleeves, and he gave in. A few moments later, wearing his new coat, he was sitting on his old one and tugging off his shoes and his thin socks.

"Socks first," I said, handing him a thick, scratchy roll.

He hesitated. His bare feet looked so white and so cold that my own toes curled in sympathy. "No man wants to lend his socks to someone else," he said. "He'd never want them back."

"Fine. Don't give them back. My father won't mind." My father wouldn't mind because he didn't even know he owned this particular pair. I'd bought them as a rather uninspired Wintermoon gift. "Jake. *Put them on.*"

Either my tone convinced him or he was too cold and tired to argue. He pulled on the socks, then laced up the boots, then rose to his feet. Unfashionable it may have been, and too big for him it definitely was, but the long dark coat gave Jake some needed weight and a certain air of grace. He looked taller, broader, older, and very, very serious.

"I wish you would let me pay you something," he said.

I stamped my foot, almost bruising it against the iron-hard earth. "It's just a stupid extra coat!" I exclaimed. "You don't owe me anything!"

"Still, I should—"

"Shovel the walk, then! Chop some firewood. My grandparents will be delighted."

"Yes, but you're the one who—"

I was so *furious*. He was so *stupid*. I gave him impossible tasks. "Make me a necklace of icicles."

"I meant something I could actually—"

"Find roses in the snow. Write me a poem." Why had I said that? I rushed on. "Bring a bluebird to breakfast."

He was silent, merely watching me with those earnest eyes. I couldn't tell if he thought I was cruel or ridiculous. "Or just say thank you," I said. "That's all that's required."

He made a stiff little motion that could have been a bow. "Thank you," he said. "Lirril. You are—thank you. This was truly kind."

Now I really did want to weep. "It wasn't kind. It was mean," I said in a muffled voice. "I just didn't want to have to feel sorry for you. So there."

Now he smiled a little. "A generous impulse born of an ungenerous thought," he said. "But I'm still warm."

"It's so unfair," I burst out.

"What is?"

"That I have—it shouldn't be that way! I have so many people who love me, and you don't have any."

"That's the way the world goes," he said.

I stared at him. If I cried, I thought my tears might freeze to my face. "But don't you want more than what you have?" I whispered.

"Of course I do," he replied. "I want a place where I fit in, people who love me, friends who come when I cry for help. I want to do work that matters, make a home that's full of happiness. I want to be the friend who goes to others when they call out. I want all those things. Who doesn't? Maybe I'll find them in Thrush Hollow. I haven't given up. I'm going to keep looking."

My mouth had formed a little *O*, and I stared at him by ragged firelight. Who would have expected such a passionate speech from the taciturn Jake? He must have realized how much he astonished me, for his face softened as he looked down at me.

"And what do you want, Lirril? What wishes did you tie to the Wintermoon wreath?"

Everything I had ever wanted in my life now seemed trivial and trite. Trevor to notice me. My friends to envy me. My parents to buy me explicit and expensive presents. "I wished—just—for little things," I stammered.

"That man," he said. "The one you didn't want to see at the ball. Did you wish for him to fall in love with you?"

Nothing so specific, though it had been Trevor's face I envisioned when I wrapped the ribbon around the wreath. "Even if I did, he never will," I said. "He's very fond of another girl."

"You don't need to worry," Jake said. "You probably have no idea how many others are just standing ready, waiting for you to notice them."

It was so untrue that I had to laugh. "When I'm back in Wodenderry, I'll look around," I said.

After that, strangely, it was easy to talk to Jake. He told me a little about his father, a somewhat feckless man who had painted lovely landscapes and sold them for pennies. I told him about my own father, filled with such laughter, and my mother, whose standards of honesty I had always found it hard to live up to. Jake liked music but did not know how to dance; I was an excellent dancer but could not play an instrument if it would save me from hanging. We had nothing in common and yet, somehow, much to discuss. I was a little shocked when my grandfather pushed through the kitchen door, the wreath in his hands. Midnight already? My grandmother was right behind him, carrying mugs of hot tea.

"Gracious, it's cold out here!" she exclaimed, as if we might not have noticed. "Here, I brought something to warm you both up."

We gratefully gulped the steaming liquid, and then Jake set down his cup so he could help my grandfather hoist the greenery onto the fire. The flames shot up, greedy for a taste of our heartfelt desires. I saw my embroidered ribbon turn to red fire, to black cinder, to gray smoke. My dreams of romance drifted through the star-scattered sky and crossed the face of the wide-eyed moon.

"That was a good wreath," my grandfather said approvingly. "There'll be a lot of wishes come true next year."

"You two go on into the house," my grandmother said. "We'll watch the fire 'til dawn."

"Are you sure?" Jake asked. "It's so cold. I could come back out in a few hours and spell you."

'They always stay out from midnight 'til morning," I said, stepping up to my grandfather and kissing his cheek. "May all your Wintermoon wishes come true," I murmured in his ear. He replied in kind.

Then I kissed my grandmother's soft skin, and we exchanged wishes as well. I was so cold and so tired that I wasn't absolutely certain I could cross the lawn and find my way back inside the inn. I yawned and my grandmother gave me a little push toward the door.

"Go in, now," she repeated. "You're about to fall asleep on your feet. Oh, and show Jake to his room! He's on the second floor, in the green room."

I nodded and hurried for the house, Jake behind me. Candles awaited us in the kitchen, and we carried them upstairs, their flames wavering against the hands that we had lifted to shield them. The green room was right off the stairwell, a big and cheerful chamber with the most comfortable mattress in the house. Still yawning, I pointed out the amenities.

"If you need anything else, the rest of us all sleep on the top floor. No one gets up much before noon, but you can help yourself to food in the kitchen tomorrow morning. If there's a commotion any time, don't worry—it'll probably be my family arriving from Wodenderry. My father has a loud voice. That's how you'll know it's him."

Jake had set his candle down on the dresser across the room, and now he was watching me with those grave, intent eyes. "Thank you so much for everything you've done," he said.

I shook my head, too tired to argue. "I didn't do anything."

I turned for the door, but he surprised me by catching my arm and turning me back to face him. Bending slightly, he blew out my candle, so that we were standing in nearly total darkness. I looked up, surprised, and he took the opportunity to kiss me. His mouth was warm. His hands, raised to cup my cheeks, were cold. Fire and moonlight.

I pulled back, too amazed to say anything, either to scold or flirt. Even in the darkness, I could tell he was laughing silently. "Good night, Lirril," he said. "May all your Wintermoon wishes come true."

The noonday sun came through my bedroom window the next day with such force that it seemed to be muscling its way into the house. I lay drowsing in my bed a few moments, allowing myself to slowly remember the evening before. Wintermoon. My grandmother's richly satisfying meal. The glacial vigil at the bonfire. With Jake. Who had kissed me at the door just before I ran out of his room—

Well, that might make for an awkward moment or two at the dining room table. I felt a small smile play around my mouth. Jake would be more embarrassed than I. He would expect me to be angry or distant or cool. Instead, I would treat him exactly as I had at dinner the night before, as if he were a not very interesting stranger. He would not know what to think by the time he left on the stage for Thrush Hollow.

That made my smile disappear. I had forgotten. Jake would be moving on as soon as the roads were clear. He wouldn't be staying in Merendon long enough for me to tease him.

Well, who cared, anyway? Stupid old Jake. Sad, stupid, misfit Jake. It wouldn't bother me if I never saw him again.

Sounds and smells from downstairs convinced me that my grandmother was up and cooking. My room was cold, so I rose, washed, and dressed in the fastest possible time. As I skipped down the steps, I glanced at the door to Jake's room, visible from the stairwell. It was closed, and I gave a little sniff. Still sleeping, like a man with no responsibilities or appointments. No ties, no one depending on him, not even his uncle eager to see him. No wonder he had no incentives to get out of bed.

My foot had just touched the floor at the bottom of the steps when my grandfather called to me. "Lirril, come see this! I'm so tickled."

I followed the sound of his voice to the parlor, where the Wintermoon gifts were stacked before the fireplace. I had put my own out the night before, and, as was tradition, my grandparents had added theirs to the pile while the rest of the house lay sleeping. There were dozens of presents laid out before the fire, and there would be dozens more by the time my parents, my aunt, and my uncle made their own contributions.

My grandfather was holding up a wide, flat board, and it took me a moment to recognize it. "Look at this," he said, and turned it so I could see the other side. It was the Leaf & Berry sign, lovingly repainted, the red words laid in crisply against a stark white background, small curlicues decorating the four corners.

I came closer to admire it. "When did you have time to do that?" I asked. The oily, pleasant smell of fresh paint drifted to my nose.

"I didn't! I'm guessing it was that young man. He must have stayed up all night to do this."

I felt my face suddenly heat with an unidentifiable emotion. "Jake? Did this? Last night after we were all in bed?" I remembered that he told me he had done painting and staining for the carpenter in Oakton. But I hadn't expected this.

"Must have," my grandfather said, turning the sign this way and that as if to detect hidden subtleties. "Or even while Hannah and I were watching the fire. He cleared the walks, too, front and back."

I felt a shiver go down my back. Which of the other tasks that I had suggested to him had he also decided to accomplish? "That's—well. What a nice thing for him to do," I said.

My grandfather nodded toward the pile of gifts. "He left you something, too. I didn't open it, of course."

My eyes were pulled irresistibly to the bounty laid out on the hearth. In all that welter, I instantly spotted it—a scroll bound with what looked like a shoelace. My name had been carefully lettered on a scrap of paper. What would I find inside? A necklace made of icicles?

"I've got to go thank him again," my grandfather said, carrying the sign toward the kitchen.

"I think he's still asleep."

"No, he's out back, chopping firewood for your grandmother. I must say, I do like that boy," my grandfather said, and disappeared through the swinging door.

There was no way I could keep myself from dropping to the floor and untying the makeshift ribbon. I unrolled the single sheet of paper. In handwriting that I instantly knew was Jake's, I found a poem. I read it as if I were gulping it down.

> *Longest night, and coldest, of the year.*
> *Lights beat back the blackness of the sky:*
> *Bonfire blazes, jubilantly garish;*
> *Full moon rises, perfect as a pearl.*
> *I do not know what fortune brought me here—*
> *Good or ill—and yet I know that I*
> *Will not forget, until the day I perish,*
> *Wintermoon, and the kindness of a girl.*

I could not breathe. My cheeks were so hot I thought they might scald my fingers if I touched my own skin. I read the poem again.

I heard voices and I leapt to my feet, not sure where to lay the poem so no one could see it, not sure how to hold my hands or what expression to summon to my face. But the voices stayed outside, as my grandfather and Jake came around to the front of the inn and began to discuss the best way to hang the fresh sign. A minute after they decided the old hooks would work just fine, my grandfather was hailed by a new voice.

"Hullo there, Bob! Warm Wintermoon to you and yours!" It was Adam Granger, who owned a tannery a few streets over. He was getting a little frail with age, and there was some talk he might be hiring a younger man to take over his business soon. "Your grandson in town yet?"

"No, he and the girls are coming in a few days. Maybe longer, if the roads aren't clear."

"That's too bad. I had some work I needed done over at the house and I was hoping to hire Renner for a few hours."

"Jake, here, he's good with his hands," my grandfather said. "What do you want done?"

"Oh, I need a couple windows reframed and there's a table that's missing a leg. Small things, but I recall that your grandson helped me out last summer, so—"

"I can do all that," Jake spoke up. His voice was quiet and confident. He didn't sound like a man who had stayed up all night, thinking up ways to show people his appreciation.

Adam sounded pleased. "Really? I got two, three more things like that you could do if you had the time."

"Stage to Thrush Hollow probably won't be through 'til tomorrow or the day after," my grandfather said. "Good chance for you to earn a little extra money."

"When could you come over?" Adam asked.

"Soon as the sign's hung," Jake replied. "Give me a minute."

I felt myself start to breathe again. Adam could come up with a million tasks for a strong young man to do. Jake might not be taking the first stage out of Merendon after all, even if it came tomorrow.

I heard some clattering above the front door as the sign was put in place, and then the fading sound of voices as Jake and Adam walked down the street. I crossed to the front window to watch them go, but all I could see was Jake's back, slim but somehow sturdier in my father's rejected coat.

My grandmother stepped into the parlor just as my grandfather came in through the front door, bringing icy air with him. "Well, I was about to ask where everyone's gone off to," my grandmother said. "I've got a meal almost ready. Where's Jake?"

"Headed out with Adam Granger to do a few chores. Seemed mighty happy at the idea of earning a few coins, too," my grandfather said.

My grandmother looked pleased. "Now, that's good for both of them," she said. "I do like that young man. Did you see all that wood he split and set up against the door? You're not going to have to lift an axe all winter."

My grandfather grinned. "Fine by me. I've got a few chores of my own I can set Jake to when he's done at Adam's."

I looked up at that, feeling even more hopeful. My hand was behind my back, holding the poem so no one could see it, but I had a feeling that my grandfather knew what I was hiding, anyway. My grandmother almost certainly realized I was concealing something, and could guess that it was a token of someone's affection. She had probably even figured out whose. She was very good at sorting out secrets.

"Do you think Jake'll stay, then?" my grandmother asked. "Here in Merendon?"

My grandfather glanced at me and he almost laughed. "Oh, I think he might," he answered. "If we give him a little encouragement."

My grandmother nodded. "I'm going to set the table. Lirril, you can run out and check the ashes if you like. See if anything's survived the fire."

"Oh—yes—that is—I will," I said, and they both turned away to hide their smiles at my disjointed speech. I waited 'til they were out of the room, then carefully rolled up my poem and tied it with the shoelace. Grabbing my coat from the hall closet, I hurried through the kitchen and out into the cold air, which was not at all warmed by the cheerful sunshine. Shivering a little, I knelt beside the coals and began sorting through the remains of the bonfire.

I was really only looking for one thing, and I found it almost immediately—the small metal button from Jake's shirt. The heat of the fire had contorted it to a strange shape and darkened its shiny surface, but it was whole, recognizable, too stubborn to give way to neglect and misuse. I cleaned it in the snow and slipped it into my pocket. I would only give it back if Jake thought to ask for it, but I was sure he wouldn't.

The button had carried a wish that wasn't mine, but I could make it come true.

# About the Author

Sharon Shinn has been part of the science fiction and fantasy world since 1995, when she published her first novel, *The Shape-Changer's Wife*, which won the Crawford Award. In 2010, the *Romantic Times* gave Shinn the Career Achievement Award in the Science Fiction/Fantasy category, and in 2012, *Publisher's Weekly* magazine named *The Shape of Desire* one of the best science fiction/fantasy books of the year. Three of her novels have been named to the ALA's lists of Best Books for Young Adults (now Best Fiction for Young Adults). She has had books translated into Polish, German, Spanish, and Japanese. She can be found at sharonshinn.net and facebook.com/sharonshinnbooks.

# About the Publisher

This book is published on behalf of the author by the Ethan Ellenberg Literary Agency.
https://ethanellenberg.com
Email: agent@ethanellenberg.com

www.ingramcontent.com/pod-product-compliance
Lightning Source LLC
Chambersburg PA
CBHW070651100726

47907CB00007B/2167